SHERIFF OF CROW COUNTY

They didn't know that the man they left for dead was Ethan Hawkesbury, the legendary lawman known as the Buscadero. But they soon would! Greenwood was a wide-open town run by a corrupt sheriff in the pay of Jackson Quinn, the wealthy owner of the Circle Q ranch. Ethan had retired to run a horse ranch, but Quinn's men put an end to that. With his future gone, Ethan took up badge and gun and set about cleaning up the town . . .

Books by Alan C. Porter
in the Linford Western Library:

CORDOBA'S TREASURE
RIVERBOAT
HIGH MOUNTAIN PERIL
PIKE'S LAW
THE LEGEND LIVES ON

A4

ALAN C. PORTER

SHERIFF OF CROW COUNTY

Complete and Unabridged

LINFORD
Leicester

First published in Great Britain in 1998 by
Robert Hale Limited
London

First Linford Edition
published 2002
by arrangement with
Robert Hale Limited
London

British Library CIP Data

Porter, Alan C.
    Sheriff of Crow County.—Large print ed.—
Linford western library
1. Western stories
2. Large type books
I. Title
823.9'14 [F]

ISBN 0–7089–9823–2

ULV 12/04/02
4 6/02

Published by
F. A. Thorpe (Publishing)
Anstey, Leicestershire

Set by Words & Graphics Ltd.
Anstey, Leicestershire
Printed and bound in Great Britain by
T. J. International Ltd., Padstow, Cornwall

To Simon and Ceri,
wishing you both a long and
happy future together.

1

He had time to reflect briefly, bitterly, that he must be getting old and maybe he wouldn't be getting any older.

The four had taken him by surprise, even though he had watched them ride up; now it was too late. With a man on each arm, the remaining two used his body as a punch bag.

Gloved fists rattled against his ribs and stomach in a methodical, merciless pattern, while from behind, a second man drove equally punishing fists into his lower back sending agonizing waves of pain flaring from his kidneys.

Blood flowed down the man's sweating face from expertly dealt punches that had split the skin above his eyes, dripping from his chin, soaking into the front of a torn, red check shirt as he sank to his knees.

A lesser man would have been

unconscious or dead long ago, but Ethan was not that man. Big-framed, only the iron-hard muscles that ridged his flat stomach saved him from serious internal injuries.

The thud of fists into his body mingled with hls own grunts and cries filled his ears.

In his mid-forties, Ethan's only admission of age lay in the thick mane of iron-grey hair and grey-flecked moustache that curled down past the corners of his mouth. With an effort he focused his closing eyes on the face above him.

The man was strongly built and lean-hipped with a mean, swarthy face and high prominent cheekbones indicating Indian or Spanish blood somewhere in the man's past. A thick black moustache decorated his upper lip, grown to take away the disfigurement of an ugly, puckered knife scar that angled down his left cheek and disappeared into the moustache. It was a face he would remember if they made the mistake of leaving him alive.

Ethan was barely hanging on to consciousness by the time the hold on him was released and he fell face down into the Montana dirt, but even then they were not finished with him.

Boot heels and toes slammed against his body, but he no longer felt any pain. A thankful numbness had spread over his bruised and battered body.

But in their final act of brutal violation he did cry out.

Heels came down viciously on the back of his hands as they clawed weakly at the hard-packed dirt. He was not sure if he felt the pain or sensed it through the numbness.

He heard a snapping noise from both hands and yelled out, turning on to his back and cradling his damaged hands against his chest.

Sunlight seared his eyes and he raised his broken, swelling hands before them, then a shadow fell across him. He opened his swollen eyes. The figure standing over him, hands on hips appeared fuzzy and out of focus, but he guessed it was the scarred man.

'You should'a lived up to your name, Hawk, an' kept on flying 'stead o' landing here. This is Circle Q land an' you're trespassing. Now git off an' stay off.' To emphasize his words, the speaker drove a toe into Ethan's side. 'If'n you show your face in Crow County again, you'll git it shot off. Git him on a horse.' The last words were not directed at him for suddenly he felt himself dragged to his feet and then bundled unceremoniously into a saddle. Unable to support himself he fell forward on to the animal's neck. His hat was rammed on to his head. 'Mind what I said, mister. Come back an' you'll be buried in Crow County.' The animal's rump was given a slap and it moved off with its barely conscious, barely alive burden.

Before unconsciousness finally claimed him, Ethan managed to turn his head enough to see thick plumes of black smoke billowing from the cabin he had built, then a dark, restful silence swallowed him up.

★   ★   ★

Jackson Quinn looked up as the door opened. In his early fifties, the thick, brushed-back mop of silver hair did little to soften the harsh lines of his square, chunky face. He leaned back from the books he had been studying and watched with bright blue eyes as Link Teal approached, spurs ringing musically with each step he took. When finally he came to a halt before the big, polished desk, Quinn barked, 'Did you get rid of him, Teal?'

'He won't be occupying Circle Q land again, Mr Quinn,' Link Teal responded casually, fingering his scarred cheek as he spoke, an automatic gesture that he did without thinking or realizing.

Quinn nodded and grunted, reaching forward and taking a cigar from a silver humidor on the desk. He made no move to offer Teal one as he clipped the end and thrust it between thick lips.

'Damn settlers think that a bit o' paper gives 'em the right to settle on my land.' He glared at Teal. 'In my day you took the land you wanted, worked it an' had no need of bits o' paper. It was yours for as far as the eye could see in any direction.'

'That's right, Mr Quinn,' Teal agreed readily, watching his boss scrape a lucifer into spluttering life along the edge of the desk and apply it to the end of his cigar. As long as Quinn continued to pay the money then he, Teal, was happy to agree to anything. 'What do you want done wi' the horses we took from Hawk? Seemed kinda shameful to let them loose, being full broke an' all?'

Quinn blew smoke and grinned, almost benignly.

'Do what you want, Teal. Look at it as a little bonus for a job well done.'

'That's mighty fair o' you, Mr Quinn. Me an' the boys 'ppreciate your kindness,' Teal responded.

Quinn glowered at Teal.

'Now don' start gitting sentimental on me, Teal.'

Before anything else could be said, the door burst open and a young man, blond hair tumbling over one eye, wheeled himself in on a creaking wheelchair. His gaze darkened as he saw Teal. He moved to the side of the desk and turned at an angle so that with just the movement of his head he could see Quinn or Teal.

'Benson tells me there's smoke coming from the eastern range. Could be that Hawk fella's in trouble.'

'So what do you want me to do 'bout it?' Quinn replied roughly.

The young man smiled, pushing the shock of hair back to reveal a lean, handsome face endowed with the same startling blue eyes as the man seated at the desk.

'Nothin', Pa. I sent Benson and a coupla the boys to take a look.'

'Ain't gonna find much,' Teal murmured with a smile.

Sam Quinn eyed Teal with obvious

distaste that dissolved into a look of horror that he transferred to his father.

'What have you done, Pa?' he demanded hotly.

Anger flared in Jackson Quinn's eyes.

'It's my land, boy, an' I do what I want on my land.'

'But it ain't your land. You never registered the eastern range,' Sam protested hotly.

'It's your pa's by right, boy,' Link Teal threw in.

Jackson Quinn rounded on the man, his earlier benign mood, gone. In its place was a hard, mean mask.

'Get the hell outa here, Teal,' he snapped. 'I know where to find you if'n the need arises.'

Teal touched the brim of his hat.

'Sure thing, boss.' His dark eyes drifted to Sam Quinn. 'See you around, boy.'

The insolent tone to his voice brought a flush of red to Sam's cheeks, but he said nothing as Teal turned his back on him and marched out.

'Why do you keep him on the payroll, Pa? He's nothin' but trouble,' Sam cried, as the door closed behind Teal. 'I'd like to throw that ranny out on his ear.' Sam's hands clenched and unclenched in anticipation of the thought.

'An' how do you propose to do that, boy, when you can't even stand on your own two feet?' Quinn demanded, instantly regretting the rashness of his tongue as he saw the look of pain sweep across Sam's face. But he did not apologize to his son. Apologies indicated weakness and lack of judgement and he had neither; besides, he did not like having his methods questioned.

'I run this spread an' I'll say who's on the payroll. One day it'll all be yours an' then you can decide. Until then . . . ' He glared at his son.

It had been a hard day for him when, five years ago, Sam had been thrown from his horse, breaking his back and losing the use of his limbs from the waist down. Almost as hard as the day, twenty years ago, he had discovered his wife in bed with his brother. Sam had been four years old at the time.

'You had Hawk run off, didn't you, Pa. Did you get Teal an' his rannies to beat up on the man?' There was no hiding the contempt in the young man's voice.

'You take care of the books, boy, an' leave me to run this spread as I see fit. Bin doing it now for more'n thirty years an' that means I know my business better'n you do.'

'There's gotta be a better way of doing business other than with fists and guns,' Sam replied.

'You gotta protect what's yours an' be seen doing it or the wolves'll move in afore you know it.'

'If'n you had registered the land properly in the first place there'd be no need of the iron-fist approach.'

'Everybody knows this land is mine,' Quinn thundered back at his son.

Sam shook his head sadly and his expression softened.

'Times are changing, Pa. It ain't good enough to know, it's gotta be legally registered in the land office or anyone can stake a claim. Hawk's the third fella you've had run off in as many years.'

'I got deeds,' Quinn replied.

'But how much do they cover?' Sam argued. 'Government's keen to get settlers out here an' if'n your deeds don't cover the area you say is yours then one day you'll be facing a whole heap o' trouble that the likes o' Link Teal won't be able to save you from.'

'You wanna make yourself useful, boy, then get down the land office an' find out why they keep selling my land to damn settlers,' Quinn snapped back.

'Maybe I'll do just that afore it gets sold out from under us,' Sam replied heatedly, and wheeled himself towards the door.

After he had gone Quinn angrily mashed out the cigar in a glass dish and wandered across to a small cabinet set against the rear wall. A collection of bottles and glasses on a silver tray stood on top. He selected a bottle of whiskey, poured himself a generous measure then moved across to a big window, glass in hand.

He stood there and stared out over the lush green land. Deeds or not, the land was his and he'd kill any man who tried to take it from him!

★　★　★

Ethan's eyes flickered open. He lay on his back, mind frighteningly blank, staring up at circular walls that flowed together in an open cone above, through which he caught a brief glimpse of the sky. A warm, heavy gloom cocooned him and the scent of pine forests filtered in, filling his nostrils, while birdsong filled his ears.

He felt a twinge of panic as he tried to identify his surroundings with a mind that refused to work. Where was he? Why was he here? Who was he? It was the latter question that bothered him the most. He couldn't remember his name.

He was covered in a blanket that had the smell of horse about it and his arms lay atop the blanket. He lifted his left hand intending to peel the blanket aside and stared at it in blank surprise when it came into view.

Small twigs had been used to splint his fingers, each bound separately and then finally all bound together to keep his fingers straight. The right hand was the same. He stared at them stupidly until a voice said, 'It would not do to clap hands, white man.'

Ethan had been so preoccupied with his splinted and bound hands that he had not heard the arrival of the newcomer. He looked up and with a sense of shock saw the buckskin-clad Indian looming over him.

'Where am I?' It took a few attempts to get his voice going and when finally it came it was a hoarse whisper.

'What do you remember?' the Indian

asked. The higher proportion of light coming through the overhead opening revealed the Indian to be an old man, hair grey, face ridged and creased.

'Nothin', dammit!' Ethan croaked and tried to lever himself up on one elbow. The effort caused him to grunt as his body exploded with pain. Sweat erupted over his face and he fell back. With the pain came memory. Everything came flooding back. The four men, the brutal beating.

The Indian smiled down at him.

'I think you do now.'

'My name's Ethan Hawk.'

'Then lie still, Ethan Hawk. Your white brothers beat you well.' He dropped into a crouch as he spoke and gently raised Ethan's head lifting a clay bowl of water to the other's dry lips. 'Drink!'

Ethan didn't realize how thirsty he was until he had drained the bowl of its warm contents. The Indian lowered his head back down then sat down cross-legged himself.

'You never answered me: where am I?' Ethan's voice was stronger now.

'Not far as the crow flies from your land. I saw what the white men did to you, then when they put you on a horse, I followed and brought you here to my tepee.'

Ethan frowned. 'Why would you do that?'

The Indian smiled. 'You treated your horses well. You seemed worth saving.'

'I'm obliged to you . . . do you have a name?'

'Running Elk, although these old bones are not much for running these days.' The old man had a wry sense of humour. He eyed Ethan with bright, black eyes. 'It was lucky for you that you are a strong man. When I first brought you here I thought you would die.'

'How long have I been here?'

'Four days.'

Ethan digested that piece of news silently.

'That's a sizeable chunk,' he mused.

'The men who attacked me: would you have any idea who they were?'

'Later we will talk again. First you must eat.' Running Elk climbed to his feet, knee joints creaking. 'I will send in White Dove.'

'I didn't think there were any tribes left here?' Ethan said in surprise, and a sad expression crossed Running Elk's face.

'There aren't. We are the only ones.' With that he ducked out of the flap and left Ethan on his own with a million unanswered questions.

White Dove came a little while later. She was a plump, moon-faced girl with long dark hair and a perpetual smile on her round, bland features. It turned out that she did not speak any English. She supported his head on one plump arm and spoonfed him a bowl of watery soup. Only when the bowl was empty did she depart.

He waited for Running Elk to reappear, but when the old man did not come, lulled by the warmth and the unending birdsong beyond the hide walls of the tepee, he fell into a doze.

He awoke suddenly to find Running Elk and White Dove looking down at him.

'Time for treatment,' Running Elk said. He turned to White Dove and said something in a language that Ethan did not understand. White Dove smiled and nodded and dropped to her knees at Ethan's side and whipped the blanket away. Much to Ethan's embarrassment he realized he was buck naked. He tried to cover his embarrassment with his splinted hands, knocking them together in his haste, groaning as stabs of pain shot from his hands.

While Running Elk looked on in amusement, White Dove gently pulled his hands away and laid them at his side.

'What's going on?' Ethan demanded.

'Indian medicine. I was shaman to my tribe.'

As he spoke, White Dove thrust her hands into a pot that Ethan had not seen before and began to apply handfuls of a grey, greasy substance, rubbing it into his bruised flesh. The smell from it was awful as it hit his nostrils.

'Jesus! What in tarnation is that?'

'Powerful medicine. Take away the pain.'

'Think I prefer the pain,' Ethan shot back.

White Dove was methodical. When she had finished his front, with the aid of Running Elk, together they turned Ethan over and the 'powerful medicine' was applied to his back, buttocks and backs of his legs. Finally he was rolled on to his back again.

'A good cigar an' bottle of whiskey woulda' been better,' Ethan said.

White Dove, still kneeling, looked up at Running Elk and said something to which the old man nodded. The next instant her hands were curled around a part of him that they had no place to be.

'Dammit, Running Elk, what's going

on?' Ethan demanded in alarm.

'White Dove wants to know if white man is as good as Indian,' Running Elk returned.

'But she can't do that,' Ethan howled, unable to do anything to stop her.

'All part of the treatment,' Running Elk replied, turning towards the flap.

'You gotta do something!' Ethan pleaded.

'Time to smoke pipe,' Running Elk replied, and ducked out of the tepee leaving the two alone.

In spite of everything, Ethan found himself rising to the occasion. Finally, satisfied all was in order, White Dove climbed to her feet, hoisted up her skirt and straddled him.

Later, much later when she had gone, Running Elk returned.

'She say you good as Indian,' he said with a grin.

'I hope you ain't figuring that I gotta marry her now?' Ethan said suspiciously.

Running Elk looked affronted.

'You get own woman. She mine. Keep an old man warm in the winter. White Dove bring food and water. Eat well and rest. Tomorrow we get you up on your feet.'

2

Sam Quinn usually enjoyed the ten-mile trip from the Circle Q to Greenwood. He loved the sweet smell of the lush grassy plains and valleys of his Montana homeland. To the east, lay the Powder River, to the west, the mighty Rockies. It was a good land where cattle grew fat and contented families raised happy children, but lately a shadow had spread across it.

It began three years ago when homesteaders began moving in on Circle Q land waving deeds of ownership, obviously an error in the Land Registry Office in Billings. Then Jackson Quinn brought in Link Teal and his crew to clear out the homesteaders. That was when he began to worry about his pa's registered ownership of the land.

Jackson Quinn was of the old school.

Tough, demanding and unmerciful in his dealings with others. He had driven the Indians off, so the land became his in his eyes and he didn't need a piece of paper to prove it!

The buckboard lurched as it crested the ridge that overlooked Greenwood causing Sam to grab at the low rail that ran around the seat.

Benson swore at the horses and checked them with the reins before giving Sam an apologetic look.

'Sorry, Sam,' he called out.

'You cain't do nothin' 'bout the trail, Pete,' Sam replied with a grin.

Below them lay the town of Greenwood, a collection of white clapboard buildings hugging either side of a wide, rutted main street dominated at the southern end by the tall church steeple. As the trail wound down and disappeared behind a stand of tall trees that edged the trail, Sam returned to his thoughts.

It was the latest incident concerning Ethan Hawk that had finally sparked him into action to find out what was going on. But first he had to find out just how much land the Circle Q officially covered compared with how much Jackson Quinn said it covered.

The land office in Greenwood was clearly in agreement with Jackson Quinn, but four days ago he had sent to Billings to get the latest official records. With that and the deeds of ownership kept at the bank, he hoped to establish once and for all the area covered by the Circle Q. The stage was due in from Billings today and with it, he hoped, his answer.

The buckboard clattered into Greenwood. The stage was not due in for a couple of hours, but Sam had other, more pleasurable, ideas of passing the time. By the time Benson had brought the buckboard to a halt outside Laura's Café, all thoughts of Circle Q problems had left his mind.

Pete Benson climbed down and hauled Sam's wheelchair from the back, then, lifting Sam like a baby, placed him gently into the wheelchair before wheeling him into the café.

There were already half-a-dozen diners there and two called out a greeting to Sam as Benson wheeled him to a corner table.

A counter ran along the rear white-painted wall fronted by a row of stools for patrons just wanting coffee. But the thing that Sam liked most was that each of the dozen or so tables that filled the available floor space, started each day clad in crisp, white linen and set with polished cutlery.

As Benson was getting him settled, a door in the rear wall at the end of the counter opened and a girl appeared.

Laura Treece was a striking-looking young woman. Just now her long raven hair was pulled back severely and tied in a ponytail at the back revealing the soft contours of her face in all its glory.

It was a face that had captivated Sam the first moment he had seen her. With its gentle, misty-green eyes and wide, smiling lips it exuded an innocence and a determination that fascinated the young man. Clad in a green dress overlaid with a white apron, she approached Sam's table, face wreathed in a welcoming smile, but her first words were not to Sam but to Pete Benson.

'Land sakes, Pete, they sure are feeding you well at the ranch.' She arched an eyebrow, the smile wider on her face. It was a gentle poke at Pete Benson's size, for he was a huge man, wide of shoulder and even wider of waist. Standing at a little over seventy-six inches tall he weighed in excess of twenty stone. But it was not flab that covered his big frame as one or two people had found out to their cost when they had taunted him about his size. He possessed an enormous strength.

It was that strength that had got him the job of looking after Sam, lifting and carrying the young man where the wheelchair would not go. It was a job that Pete enjoyed, for he was quite devoted to Sam.

Pete grabbed the hat from his head and his heavy-jowled cheeks puckered and creased in a grin.

'Reckon I do like my chow, ma'am,' he agreed.

'Will you be eating, too?' Laura enquired.

''Fraid not, ma'am. Got me some chores to do around town, but I'll be back when the stage comes in.' He looked down at Sam. 'You all right there, Sam?'

'I'll be just fine, Pete. You take your time, I couldn't be in better hands,' Sam replied.

'I'll be on my way then.' He nodded at Sam and looked at Laura. 'Ma'am!'

'See you later, Pete,' Sam called as the big man strode away, jamming the hat back on his head as he went.

Laura turned her attention to Sam.

'And what'll be your pleasure today, Sam?'

Sam eyed her with an impish grin dancing in his eyes. 'I could sure think of a thing or two an' food wouldn't come into it,' he said in a lowered voice, that brought a crimson flush to her face.

She looked around quickly, hoping that no one else had heard his words.

'Sam Quinn, what a thing to say,' she chided him softly, but there were real memories behind his words. Memories of a Sunday afternoon picnic.

With so many eligible, able-bodied young men around, it had surprised him when his own clumsy attempts at wooing her had worked. Of course, the cynics had responded that it was his money she was after and Jackson Quinn was one of those cynics. 'She's after getting her claws into the Circle Q, boy. Keep away from her,' his father had stated and that had been followed by a blazing row between the two.

Sam had not kept away from her. Instead, a growing relationship between the two had bonded them closer together.

Sam smiled up at her blushing countenance.

'Bacon, eggs an' all the trimmings, if'n you please, Miss Laura.' He decided to spare her blushes. 'Perhaps you'd care to join me for coffee later on?'

'I might just do that,' she replied crisply, and moved away to fill his order.

During the next hour or so the café filled up and while Sam ate a leisurely breakfast, Laura and her two helpers were kept busy. But, finally the early-morning rush was over and Laura appeared with a pot of coffee and joined Sam at his table. Only one customer remained and that was the overweight shape of Sheriff Floyd Tupper. He occupied a stool at the counter sipping a cup of coffee and every so often gave the two a sly look.

Sam disliked the fat sheriff. He had only got the job because Sheriff Haynes had been killed out on the trail a year ago by bushwhackers who had never been caught. It had given Jackson Quinn the opportunity to install Tupper in office, for the rancher hated anyone who opposed him and Tupper, unlike his predecessor, did as he was told and that's how Jackson Quinn liked things to be.

Tupper's loose, non-effective law-keeping had allowed a rougher element to creep into town. It was getting to the point where men on the run came to Greenwood to escape the law. The streets of Greenwood were not safe for law-abiding citizens after dark. It was said that after dark, Tupper could not be found anywhere. He took himself out of town and did not return until daybreak. It was down to the likes of Link Teal and his cronies to control the bad elements that might look to cause trouble to the Circle Q.

Sam purged thoughts of Tupper from his mind as he and Laura chatted and drank coffee, but that ended abruptly when a sneering voice broke loudly across them.

'Well if'n it ain't the lovebirds, all cosy, cosy together.'

Sam snapped his head around to find Link Teal and one of his men, Chuck Dawson, moving between the tables towards them. Dawson, a mean, lank-haired man, peeled away to hitch himself on to a stool close to Tupper.

Teal came on, hitched a chair out from under a nearby table and sprawled himself down in it facing the two.

'What do you want, Teal?' Sam snapped.

'Does your daddy know where you are, boy?' Teal countered with a leer.

'Do you even know your daddy?' Sam refused to be drawn, turning Teal's baiting game back on the man.

Teal's smile sagged a little as he fought to keep his composure.

'The boy's gotta sense of humour,' Teal called over his shoulder to Dawson.

'Need it with so many clowns about,' Sam said crisply.

Teal's face darkened. He was no

match in a battle of words.

'I think mebbe you'd better watch your mouth, boy,' he snarled menacingly.

'I'd sooner watch yours trying to form words,' Sam prodded.

Teal's eyes slitted angrily.

Laura grabbed Sam's arm.

'Please, Sam,' she pleaded, fear in her eyes.

'Reckon he's calling you a fool, boss,' Dawson spoke up, adding fuel to the fire that Teal had started and was now unable to control.

'Is that it, cripple, you calling me a fool?' He stood up and towered over Sam.

'No, Link, I ain't calling you a fool. You're too stupid to be a fool,' Sam replied.

Laura jumped to her feet. 'Stop it the pair of you.'

'I reckon you owe me an apology, cripple,' Teal hissed.

Sam felt a flutter of panic churn in his stomach as he looked up into

Teal's anger-suffused face, but his face remained calm. He realized he had pushed Teal too far, but the inherited Quinn stubbornness would not allow him to back down.

'I'll allow Link's right, boy,' Sheriff Tupper spoke up, grinning behind Teal's taut back.

'Well, boy, I'm waiting,' Teal said softly, eyes flashing, hand now resting on the ivory handle of a low-hung Colt.

'Leave him be, Teal, or you'll answer to me!'

All eyes had been fixed on the two that none had heard or seen Pete Benson enter until he spoke.

Teal spun, the Colt leaping fluidly into his hand and pointing unwaveringly at Benson's ample stomach.

'D'yer think you can beat a bullet, fat man?' Teal spat out as, unarmed, Benson came to a halt.

'More to the point, Teal, can you?' Sam called out, accompanying his words with the clicking of a hammer being thumbed back.

Laura gasped and Teal looked back over his shoulder to find that Sam had produced a Colt Pioneer from somewhere and was pointing it at his back.

A slow smile spread across his stubble-lined face.

'Well, well, the boy's carrying a hogleg. What are you gonna do wi' it, boy?'

'Mebbe make the world a better place by burying you,' Sam shot back.

'Reckon your daddy wouldn't like that. 'Sides, backshoot an' that'd be murder. What d'yer reckon, Sheriff?'

'Damn right you are, Link.' Tupper agreed, slipping off the stool. 'Best you hand that over, boy or I'll — '

'You'll do whatever Jackson Quinn says,' Sam thundered back, stopping Tupper in his tracks. 'You'll dance to whatever tune my pa plays because that's what he pays you for. Now stick your fat rump back on that stool, Tupper, or the town'll be looking for a new sheriff.'

Tupper blanched, the pomposity

knocked from him and he returned to his seat.

'I'll make damn sure your pa hears 'bout this little incident,' Tupper bleated, but Sam ignored him, eyeing Teal.

'Think ag'in, Teal. You know my pa, he don't like losers. He's always tellin me to — ' Sam gave a mirthless smile — 'stand on my own two feet. Putting a bullet in you might well impress him. Scum like you an' your crew can be bought in any saloon for a cheap bottle of rot-gut. He ain't gonna cry too much over your grave.'

The smile left Teal's face. He shoved the gun back in its holster and turned to face Sam, hands raised to shoulder level.

'Must be your lucky day, boy. No one's ever thrown down on me an' lived to tell the tale, but it suits me to bide my time.'

A thin, nasty smile twitched his lips. 'Just remember the trail can be a dangerous place, accidents can happen.'

'Don't worry, Teal, I aim to be real careful in the future.'

Teal gave him one last glowering look then turned on his heels and marched stiffly away, brushing past Pete and motioning Dawson to follow him. Dawson lingered in the doorway to give Sam a toothy grin before following Teal out into the street.

Sam lowered the gun to his lap; his hand was shaking. He looked across at Tupper.

'Ain't there somewhere you should be, Sheriff?'

Tupper slid off the stool and made for the door.

'You ain't heard the last of this,' he cried, but was gone before Sam could frame a suitable reply.

Sam relaxed back in his chair.

'Sam Quinn, that was the most stupid thing you've ever done. You coulda' been killed,' Laura scolded angrily, but all the same came around the table and hugged him. 'Stupid but brave,' she whispered, stroking his hair

35

as she crushed his face against her soft bosom.

'Well if'n it gets a fella a hug like that I might just do it again,' Sam responded when finally they disengaged.

'Don't you dare, Sam Quinn,' she remonstrated with a smile.

'Has the stage come in yet, Pete?' Sam asked.

'There weren't nothin' for you on it, Sam,' Pete replied apologetically.

Sam sighed, frustration on his face.

'Guess we'll have to wait until next week,' he said, unable to keep the disappointment from his voice.

Jackson Quinn was less than happy when Sam returned home.

'Dammit, boy, what d'yer mean by pulling iron on a man like Teal?' the old man thundered. 'You coulda' got yoursel' killed!'

'I see Tupper travels fast when it suits him,' Sam replied mildly.

'Someone's gotta keep an eye on you,' Quinn returned.

'I can handle the likes o' Teal,' Sam

replied. 'It's Tupper who worries me. The streets of Greenwood are not safe for decent folk to be on after dark. All manner of riff-raff come out of the woodwork, and Tupper, he ain't nowhere to be found.'

'Tupper does as he is told an' that's good enough for me,' Quinn barked back at his son from the other side of the desk. ''Sides, decent folk shouldn't be walking the streets at night!'

'Dammit, Pa, Greenwood was a nice town once. A place for families an' kids. Pretty soon the good folk are gonna start moving out an' there'll be nothing left but trash like Teal,' Sam shot back angrily.

'Teal an' Tupper do their jobs. How 'bout you? Did you find out who's been selling off my land, or were you too busy wi' that Treece woman?' There was no disguising the sneer in Jackson Quinn's voice and it brought a flush of anger to Sam's face.

'I had breakfast at the café,' Sam replied tight-lipped.

'That's not how I heard it.'

'I don't give a damn what you heard,' Sam responded hotly. 'And no, the copy of the land records I sent for did not arrive today, mebbe next week.'

'The woman's a golddigger. She's got her eye on the Circle Q. You mark my words, boy.' Quinn nodded sagely at his own words.

'No wonder Ma took off with Uncle Seb all those years ago,' Sam snapped, before he could stop himself.

'I told you never to mention that man's name,' Quinn hissed out, face set and hard.

'Then leave Laura and me alone,' Sam snarled back, turned his chair and propelled it towards the door. He was sorry for what he had blurted out in the heat of the moment. Jackson Quinn did not like to be reminded that his brother had taken his wife from him and had forbidden any mention of either of them. Sam knew the memories still hurt even after twenty years, but he was not about to apologize.

He wheeled himself out on to the veranda and stared out over the rolling countryside.

It was always the same: whenever he and his father spoke, it ended up in an argument.

He sighed and shook his head sadly.

3

On the same morning that Sam Quinn went into town, Ethan, supported by Running Elk and White Dove, took his first, tentative steps in almost a week. With a blanket wrapped around his waist to preserve his modesty, they helped him out of the tepee into a warm, summer morning.

To begin with, his legs were as wobbly as a newborn colt's, each step accompanied by stabs of pain lancing through his back, but he gritted his teeth and persevered.

His stubbornness not to give into the pain paid off. Within ten minutes he was walking on his own and dragging down deep breaths of pine-scented air and letting the warming rays of the sun caress his battered body still covered with areas of bruised, discoloured flesh.

Running Elk had made his home in a

high valley ringed with grey walls of rock and clothed in rich, green grass. At one end, a small pine forest provided a cool haven from the hot sun and it was here he had erected his tepee. It was close to a narrow stream that bubbled out of the rocks further back in the forest and meandered across the centre of the valley before vanishing underground.

It was an idyllic place filled with a serenity and peace that Ethan had not known before.

When, finally, Ethan felt it was time to rest his weary, aching limbs, he found a convenient log by the stream and sat down, wrapped in the mottled light that filtered down through the canopy of needles above.

Running Elk, who had been monitoring his progress, nodded his head in satisfaction.

'You heal well for a white man, Ethan,' he acknowledged, dropping down into a cross-legged position on a small grassy hump facing the other.

'But then you have had much practice.'

He let his eyes linger on Ethan's deep, broad chest that was scarred with more than half-a-dozen old wounds.

'Some,' Ethan agreed, smiling through a thickening beard stubble.

'You have the body of a warrior, not a horse dealer,' Running Elk observed shrewdly.

'Had me a lifetime of fighting other people's battles, figured it was time to settle down an' horse dealing seemed a lot safer. Guess I figured wrong.' A hard note crept into Ethan's voice. 'Those rannies who ran me off my land: do you have any idea who they were?'

'They work for the man called Jackson Quinn and their leader is called Link Teal. He is a hard, merciless man. He burned your cabin and took your horses.'

The steel in Ethan's eyes hardened and flashed.

'But he made a bad mistake,' Ethan said, and the smile that stretched his lips, but failed to reach his eyes sent a shiver through the old Indian.

'I do not understand,' Running Elk ventured hesitantly.

'He left me alive,' Ethan replied softly. He held up his splinted hands. 'When do these come off?'

'You are anxious to leave!' It was a statement rather than a question.

'I have a few problems to sort out,' Ethan replied. 'When, Running Elk?'

'Tomorrow.'

'Good.' Ethan stood up, grimacing at the pain that niggled the small of his back. 'I'll be glad to be able to pull my pants on.'

'It will be five, six day before you are well enough to leave,' Running Elk called to Ethan's retreating back.

The following day Running Elk removed the splints and with strong but gentle hands, kneaded movement back into the stiff fingers.

'These are not the hands of a horse dealer; too soft,' he said, as White Dove deposited a bowl of what looked like grey mud on the ground before Ethan who was seated on a low boulder outside the tepee. 'Body of a warrior, but the hands of a maiden. You are a strange man, Ethan Hawk.'

'The line of work I used to do called for both,' Ethan said enigmatically. 'I was a peace officer in a former life, an' my name's not Hawk, it's Hawkesbury.'

Running Elk indicated the other's scarred torso paying no heed to the name change admission.

'Not too much peace, eh?' he commented dryly.

'That's why I changed my name. New life, new name.' Ethan wrinkled his nose at the stench rising from the pot. 'I sure as hell hope that ain't breakfast.'

'Indian medicine,' Running Elk announced. 'I was shaman to my tribe. Crow shaman. Put hands in. Help to make better.'

Hesitantly, Ethan put his hands in, wincing, for the muddy goo was hot, but once he got used to it he felt the stiffness leave his finger joints though it did little for his nose.

'Dammit, Running Elk, couldn't you find something a little more sweet-smelling?' he complained, but Running Elk just smiled.

'Make hand movements like this,' he instructed, clenching and unclenching his hands.

Ethan did as he was told and by the time the 'mud' had cooled, his fingers felt supple, the joints moving without pain.

'How come you stayed when your tribe moved away?' Ethan asked later.

'Reservation no good for Indian. Need freedom.'

'An' Jackson Quinn lets you stay?'

'He would kill me if he could find me. This place not easy to find so he does not try anymore.' A mischievous imp danced in Running Elk's eyes. 'Except when I steal his cattle.'

Ethan eyed the old man in wonder.

'I wouldn't have taken you for a cattle rustler, Running Elk.'

'A man must eat and Jackson Quinn

has many cattle. Many of my people died when he drove them from this land, so I avenge their memories by taking a few cattle. The winters are cold. Need meat for food and hide for clothes.'

Ethan nodded. 'Reckon he owes you that at least. What about White Dove, she don't look like a Crow squaw?'

'She Sioux. Run away from reservation seven summers ago. I found her wandering in the mountains. Now she stay with me.'

Five days later, Ethan rode out of the mountains on the dappled-grey mare that had carried him in. His clothes had been washed and repaired and White Dove had given him a tan and white hide jacket that she had made during his stay. He strongly suspected it came from a Circle Q cow and that made it all the more appropriate.

He was a different man from two weeks ago. His hair was longer and now a curly, grey-splashed beard accompanied the moustache. The beard made him look older, but he decided to keep it for now.

He rode across the grassy plain of the high ridge to where the burnt-out remains of his cabin lay and dismounted before it.

Cabin, barn; Teal and his crew had been thorough, burning everything to the ground until all that remained was a section of charred corral fencing.

Tethering the grey, Ethan entered the ruins of the cabin. Only the wooden floor had survived and that was black and blistered. In places the boards had sprung away from the wooden joists below where the heat had warped them. He moved to a point that was left of the centre of the room and began kicking away the pile of ash.

A metal handle appeared, folded into a recess. Ethan bent, gripped the handle and pulled and a trap-door opened. A layer of fine ash slid from the opening door and sent up a black cloud that filled his nostrils with acrid, tickling particles. Ethan stepped back and let the cloud settle a little before kneeling down and reaching into the opening.

It was not very deep or wide, but big enough for a bulky carpet bag that he hauled up into the light of day. The secret recess was something he had used before to keep valuable items in other places he had lived.

He carried the bag back to where the grey grazed the long grass. There he opened it and took out a roll of bills. It was not that he distrusted banks, most of his cash lay in the Bank of Greenwood, but sometimes a man needed money in a hurry, so he always kept a.thousand dollars on hand.

Pocketing the roll, he stared for a while down at the contents of the bag before closing it up again.

In the bag lay his past and now it looked as though it was to be his future, too!

It was late in the afternoon that Ethan rode into Greenwood. He had bought supplies in the town when he had first moved in, but his visits had never been protracted and now with the beard he doubted that anyone would recognize him.

He rode the length of main street to the livery stable at the far end of town noting that already the shops and stores were closing up for the night. He frowned, puzzled; it seemed to him a mite early to be closing. In all the towns he knew the stores remained open well after dark.

He reined in at the livery stable and slid wearily from the saddle feeling stiffer than he expected. It was while he was kneading the cricks from his back that the old man scurried from the stable towards him.

Thin and bony, clad in grubby old range clothes that looked a size too big for him, the oldster came to a halt before him. Bald as a coot, but what he lacked in hair he made up for in a wild, straggly red beard. Above the startling beard, tangled here and there with bits of straw, the walnut-wrinkled face contained a pair of sparkling, button-black eyes.

'Kin I help you, stranger? Handle's Rusty on account o' these 'ere chin whiskers an' I own the livery stable.' There was a rasp to the reedy tone of his voice that flowed out over almost toothless gums.

Ethan smiled. 'Need to bed my horse for the night.'

'Then you come to the right place,' Rusty chuckled. 'Bring her along an' we'll get her fed, watered an' bedded down.'

Ethan, leading the grey, followed Rusty into the stable. Inside, the warm, still air was rich with the smell of hay and horse droppings. The grey's metal-shod hooves rang on the stone flags of the central aisle. One side was piled high with hay, the other side sectioned into a dozen stalls of which about half were occupied. Ethan was pleased to note that the stalls not in use had been cleaned out.

The old man stopped at a middle

stall and Ethan led the grey in and proceeded to unsaddle it.

'You keep a good stable, Rusty,' Ethan commented.

'Any hoss here gets the best treatment,' Rusty spoke up proudly. 'Them critters have saved my hide more'n once in the past, so they deserve to be looked after.'

Ethan threw the saddle and blanket over the stout wooden panel that separated the stalls. He paused to stroke the animal's muzzle before gathering up his bag and stepping from the stall to let Rusty close the gate.

'Closes up early around here,' Ethan commented.

'Didn't at one time. Greenwood was a good place to be once, but times change.'

'Obviously not for the better.'

'Town's gone to pot since the regular sheriff got his'sel' shot an' Floyd Tupper took over.' Rusty scowled and leaned on the gate. 'He lets any saddle bum and drifter in an' don' give a hoot what they gets up to. Locks up his office o' a night an' hightails to a shack he owns down by the river, coupla miles east o' here. Comes back in the morning. What kinda law is that?' He glared at Ethan as though it was his fault.

'How come he gets away with it?'

''Cause he works for Jackson Quinn. Does what he's told an' that's all ol' man Quinn cares about. That's why the stores close up early. Greenwood ain't a place to be after sundown. That's when the hellions take over an' decent folk lock an' bolt their doors an' don' venture out till sun-up.' Rusty paused and scowled up at Ethan. 'You look kinda familiar. Have I seen you afore?'

'Just rode into town tonight,' Ethan replied. 'Can you recommend a place to stay?'

'Hotel down the street apiece. Jake Toomey's place, opposite the Silver Wheel saloon. Staying long?'

'Long enough,' Ethan replied enigmatically.

'Looking for work?'

'You offering?'

'Circle Q's hiring. Got a big round-up coming off an' they're looking for drovers, that's if'n you're interested.'

'I'll bear it in mind.'

'You on the run, mister?' The question came out of the blue from Rusty, its candour surprising Ethan.

'That's sure one helluva question to ask a man, Rusty.'

'Ain't saying running from the law,' Rusty defended. 'Man could be on the run from a nagging wife, the husband of someone else's wife. Could jus' be plumb tired o' life where he came from an' is looking for somethin' new.'

'How'd you see me?' Ethan prompted, a smile tugging at his lips.

Rusty toyed with his beard thoughtfully.

'Cain't rightly say, that's why I was asking. Floyd Tupper'll be asking when he sees you. He has to report any strangers in town to ol' man Quinn.'

'An' what happens if'n Quinn don't like what he hears?'

'He sends some o' the hard cases he's got working for him to persuade the stranger he ain't welcome, an' mister, if'n he sets Link Teal on you, take the advice of an ol' man an' get outa town quick.' Rusty's head bobbed.

'He's one of the hardcases is he?'

'Don' come any harder. He's got three others wi' him. Dawson, Roach an' Stiles. Real mean rannies.' Rusty shuddered at the thought. 'I ain't skeert o' no man, but them four, now they's a different pack o' coyotes. They run the town while Tupper's jus' the front man an' Quinn's errand boy.'

Ethan shook his head in disgust. 'Doesn't anyone care about the town?' he asked.

'Sure. Sam Quinn, he's Jackson Quinn's son an' a real nice fella, he'd like to clean this town out an' stand it back on its feet.'

'Then why don't he?'

''Cause he can't stand on his own

feet. Bruk his back in a riding accident five year ago an' ain't walked since. Gets around in one o' them there chairs on wheels an' a body cain't do much from one o' those.'

'No one else? Mayor, civic dignitaries?'

'Ain't no one in this town who ain't been bought an' paid by Jackson Quinn. He votes you in an' he votes you out if'n you don't do like he wants. Only other fella I seen stand up to Quinn is Doc Blanchard.' Rusty chuckled. 'Speaks his mind does Doc.'

'Seems to me that makes two of you,' Ethan said dryly.

'Turned seventy-five this year an' when a man gets that old, speaking his mind is all that's left.'

'Anyone else?'

'Bob Brady, runs the Boxed B spread south of town. He an' Quinn don't get on too well. Say, for a stranger, you ask an awful lotta questions.'

'Pays a man to know something of the town he's going into,' Ethan replied.

'Take good care of the mare, she means a lot to me, an' look after my saddle.'

'Don' you worry none 'bout horse an' saddle. Say, you gotta name besides 'stranger'?'

'Ethan.'

'Well Ethan, you take care. Man wi'out a hogleg on his hip can sure find himself in trouble.'

Ethan hefted his bag.

'I'll remember that.' He turned away and headed out into the lengthening shadows of approaching night.

Later, Ethan stood at the window of his hotel room that overlooked the main street and the Silver Wheel saloon. The only light in the room was that thrown out by the saloon, enough to pick out the old dressing-table and outlines of the bed and his own shadow cast on the rear wall.

Earlier in the evening he had seen the sheriff leave his office that lay to the left of the saloon and ride out, giving the town to the roughs and drunks to do with as they willed.

The sounds from the saloon filtered through the fly-specked glass of the window; coarse laughter, shouting, an occasional female shriek, all overlaid with the discordant tinkling of a piano badly in need of tuning.

Drunks staggered from the saloon to urinate in the road. Gunshots peppered the night as cowboys fired off their pistols just for the hell of it.

Ethan sipped a glass of whiskey as a fist fight erupted in the road below and customers streamed from the saloon to hoorah the protagonists and lay bets on who would win.

Girls appeared on the narrow veranda that fronted the upper storey of the saloon. They wore very little in the way of clothing as they shouted down to the crowd.

The whole sordid scene was one he had witnessed in many cow towns, but usually it was broken up by the local sheriff. Here in Greenwood there was no such control.

Ethan downed his whiskey in a gulp

and drew the thin curtains before lighting the lamp.

They had beat him near to death, run him off his land, stolen his horses and burned down his cabin. Now he was ready to return the compliment.

He stared down at the bed that was spread with the contents of his bag, a dark suit and blue shirt, both crumpled and creased from their long stay in the bag. They would need to be cleaned and pressed before he wore them again. A chestnut-brown gunbelt lay coiled next to them with the walnut butt of an Adams double-action revolver poking from the holster. Next to the gunbelt lay a single-barrelled shotgun, its barrel shortened to half its length. By the side of the bed stood a pair of black boots. These had been polished until they shone, likewise the gun holster had been lightly oiled to soften and make the leather supple.

Ethan sighed and dipped into the bag for the last item. It was a five-pointed star in a metal circle. The clothes, gun and star had made him a legend in a dozen towns across the west and earned him the name, 'Buscadero'. A hard, gun-toting lawman.

He had come to Montana to bury the past, spend his twilight years raising horses, he had even part-changed his name for an anonymity that would leave him in peace, but now it seemed that the past was not willing to let the legend die.

He couldn't make up his mind if he regretted it or not, but he did know that someone would!

4

Sheriff Floyd Tupper usually enjoyed his first coffee of the day in Laura's café, but today Doc Blanchard had caught up with him.

'What are you gonna do 'bout the no-good rannies who take over the town at night, Tupper?' he demanded. Doc Blanchard was a short, stocky individual clad in a crumpled brown suit. Beneath the wide-brimmed slouch hat he wore, his face was a mask of anger.

Tupper groaned. 'Dammit, Doc, can't a fella enjoy his coffee in peace?'

'Little Molly Blake was standing at her window last night when a bullet from a drunkard's gun damn near tore her arm off.'

'She shoulda been in bed not staring outa windows,' Tupper replied indifferently from a stool at the counter.

'Is that all you gotta say?' Doc exploded.

'What d'yer expect me to say?'

'I expect you to be here when drunks are shooting off their guns, an' put a stop to it.'

Tupper scowled at Doc.

'Quit your bellyaching, Doc. Likely give a man a headache wi' you jawing in his ear.'

'Dammit, Tupper, you're supposed to uphold the law here, not run out on it.'

Tupper swung round on the stool to face him.

'Lookit here, Doc. I don' tell you how to do your horse doctoring so you don' tell me how to do my job.'

'Horse doctoring!' Doc shouted. 'By heck, Tupper, one o' these days you might need some of my horse doctoring an' I surely look forward to that day.'

'You surely try a man's patience, Doc. If'n you keep it up I'm gonna have to run you in for a breach of the peace, *my* peace.'

'Yeah, that's about your level, Tupper.

You'd lock an innocent man up an' let the scum of the earth walk the streets free.'

Tupper's face reddened, but before he could reply, a man burst into the café and headed straight for him.

'Better rouse up, Sheriff. There's a fella in your office an' he's tossed all your belongings out on to the sidewalk.'

Tupper jerked upright on the stool.

'You still drunk from last night, Tooley?'

'Best see for yourself, Sheriff.'

Coffee forgotten, Tupper slid from the stool.

'Too right I will an' if'n this is some fool joke o' yours, Tooley, you'll be spending the rest of the day behind bars.'

'Ain't no joke, Sheriff,' Tooley replied.

A smile had flooded Doc's face.

'This I gotta see. Hold the coffee, Laura, I'll be back.' As Doc followed Tupper out, the dozen or so eaters who had been enjoying the altercation between the two, jumped up and eagerly followed on.

By the time Tupper reached his office, the crowd in his wake had doubled in size. Tupper took one look at his belongings scattered over the sidewalk, pulled his pistol and marched into his office.

A big, broad-shouldered man stood with his back to the door. He was clad in a dark suit and low-crowned stetson and wore shiny black boots.

'I dunno who you are, mister, but you've done enough to earn yousel' a spell in jail. Now git them hands up!' Tupper thumbed back the hammer of his Colt.

Ethan turned slowly from a map of the territory he had been studying and faced Tupper. The first thing Tupper saw was the badge gleaming on the stranger's left lapel. The next was the cold, hard eyes that stared at him.

'You've been replaced, Tupper. Hand in the badge and get out!'

Tupper felt his insides tighten.

'Mr Quinn never said anythin' 'bout replacing me,' he said thickly.

'Then you'll be able to tell him when you see him,' Ethan replied smoothly. 'The name's Hawkesbury, E. J. Hawkesbury; you may have heard of me?'

Tupper's eyes widened at the name and a sudden tightness gripped his chest.

'You're the one they call the Buscadero,' he said faintly.

'I'm glad you've heard of me. Now I've got a bit of advice for you: never hold a gun on a man unless you intend using it.'

A sweat broke out over Tupper's face and the gun in his hand shook.

Doc, who had edged into the office, said softly, 'Might get to use my horse doctoring after all.'

Tupper, with more courage than had been accredited to him, replied, 'You ain't got no jurisdiction here.' There was a tremble in his voice.

Ethan's lips twitched in a cold smile. 'Jurisdiction goes to the man who pulls the trigger first,' he said calmly. 'Do you think you can pull the trigger quicker than I can draw and fire?' Ethan's hands had been thumb-tucked in the front of his gunbelt, now his right hand dropped down to hang beside his holstered Adams.

Panic flared through Tupper. He had heard stories about this man's prowess with a gun and the speed of his draw and facing him, looking into those calm, unafraid eyes, he had no reason to doubt their truth.

'I ain't shooting!' Tupper cried, uncocking the Colt and returning it to its holster. He followed this by removing his sheriff's star and tossing it on to the top of the battered desk.

'Dammit!' Doc complained. 'I was looking forward to digging a bullet or two outa you.'

Tupper ignored Doc, turning his palms to Ethan and backing away.

'Guess we'll see what Mr Quinn has to say 'bout this. He ain't gonna like it.'

'I'm sure he won't,' Ethan agreed.

Tupper reached the door, turned and stumbled through it. His exit was the signal for the crowd to break up and start spreading the news. Only Doc remained behind staring thoughtfully at Ethan.

'So you're the famous Buscadero, eh?'

'Do you have a problem with that?' Ethan enquired.

'Nope.' Doc massaged the back of his neck. 'I've heard it said that you ain't nothin' but a legalized gunman an' no better'n the rannies you go after. On the other hand, you've also been called a hero. Name's Doc, Doc Blanchard.' Doc had moved forward as he spoke, now he stuck out a welcoming hand.

Ethan took the hand and shook it before shrugging his shoulders.

'Depends which side of the law you're on. Say, you don't happen to be related to Rusty down at the livery stable. He's a man who tends to speak his mind as well.'

Doc chuckled.

'Guess you can call it the privilege of old age.' He shook his head with a woeful look on his face. 'Jackson Quinn ain't gonna take kindly to you kicking his pet sheriff outa office an' taking over.'

'I'm counting on it,' Ethan replied enigmatically causing Doc's bushy eyebrows to rise, but he did not pursue the subject.

'Well if'n ever a town needed the talents of a man like you, Sheriff, this is the town, but I can't help thinking that you might have bitten off more'n you can chew. You'll find that Jackson Quinn tends to stick in the craw. He's a tough old boy, but the men who ride with him are tougher still.'

'I'll bear that in mind, Doc.'

Doc took a watch from his pocket and stared at it.

'Damn! I should'a been somewhere else ten minutes ago. I'll try an' be around when Quinn rides into town.'

★ ★ ★

67

The hour ride to the Circle Q Tupper cut by half by pushing his horse forward at a punishing rate. By the time horse and rider reached the ranch, both were sweating profusely.

Jackson Quinn was stood by the corral when Tupper brought his mount to a sliding halt and jumped from the saddle and ran towards Quinn.

'Dammit, Tupper, what in tarnation's got into you? You've damn near killed that horse. Where's your star?' Quinn glared at Tupper.

'Damn fella threw me outa my office, took my badge an' says he's sheriff now,' Tupper babbled, pulling a square of dirty rag from his pocket and mopping his damp brow.

Jackson Quinn stared dumbfounded at Tupper.

'If'n you're drunk, Tupper, an' need to be sleeping off the likker dreams . . . ?'

'I ain't, Mr Quinn.' Quickly Tupper rattled out the chain of events that had led him a breakneck ride to the Circle Q.

Quinn listened, at first with disbelief, then with a growing anger.

'The damn you say!' he growled when Tupper brought his jaw to a rest. 'We'll soon see 'bout this. Nobody takes over anything in my town without my say-so. Corrigan, round up a dozen men.'

'You don' understand, Mr Quinn,' Tupper broke in. 'The man's E. J. Hawkesbury, the one they call the Buscadero.'

'Never heard of him,' Quinn replied.

'You would've if'n you'd been down Arizona way ten years back.' Corrigan, a short, thickset man with a permanent scowl spoke up. 'Clearsville was one helluva town on the Arizona, New Mexico border. I was there when he single-handedly cleaned that town up.' Corrigan shuddered. 'In just a week he had tamed that town an' it looked like an army had fought a battle there, not one man on his own.'

'I see'd him do the same thing in Bitter Springs, Colorado,' Slim Baxter volunteered. 'Killed over twenty men in a single shoot-out. That was five years ago. The Buscadero ain't someone you argue with. You do what he says or die.'

There were solemn nods all round from the half-dozen cowboys who had heard Tupper's story.

'I heard he'd retired,' someone called.

'Well he ain't now,' Tupper snapped back.

'Well, he's sure gonna wish he had,' Jackson Quinn said darkly. 'Get the men together, Corrigan, we'uns got some visiting to do.'

'I ain't riding on the Buscadero,' Corrigan said flatly, causing Quinn's face to darken.

'You'll ride wi' me, Corrigan, or you're finished at the Circle Q.'

'Guess it's time I was moving on anyway,' Corrigan replied and turned away, heading for the bunkhouse.

Quinn rounded on the remaining men.

'Any more o' you lily-livered rannies

fixing to run out on me?'

'Well, I ain't skeered o' this *hombre*. I'm with you, Mr Quinn. Ain't no man bigger than the bullet that kills 'im.' Jeb Lacey, a big-built, arrogant cowboy spoke up, a smirk on his stubblelined face.

'That's what I like to hear,' Quinn praised.

'Shouldn't we get Link an' his boys to handle this one?' a nervous voice questioned.

'I run this ranch an' the town, not Teal,' Quinn thundered. 'Get your horses an' a fresh one for Tupper here.'

Floyd Tupper looked unhappy at the idea.

'Shouldn't I wait here, Mr Quinn?'

'You ride wi' us, Tupper, or you join Corrigan, is that clear?'

'Clear, Mr Quinn,' Tupper agreed heavily.

Jackson Quinn had returned to his study and was buckling on a gunbelt when Sam rolled himself into the room. He took one look at his grim-faced father and consternation flared across his handsome features.

'What's going on, Pa?'

'Some damn stranger has thrown that fool Tupper out of his office an' settled himself in as sheriff.'

Sam's eyes widened at the thought.

'So what are you gonna do?'

'Throw him out!' Jackson Quinn declared brusquely and left the room leaving a bemused Sam staring after him.

★　★　★

Soon after Doc had departed, Ethan left the confines of the office and strolled at a leisurely pace down the wide main street of Greenwood.

News of his arrival had travelled fast and he passed little groups of people who eyed him in silent curiosity. He entered the Silver Wheel saloon. It was mostly empty now and a swamper was cleaning the floor before the long bar.

'Well, well, so it's true what I heard?'

a voice drawled.

Ethan turned. A man sat at a baize-topped table to the right of the batwings. Before him, cards were spread out in a half-finished game of patience. He was a slim, clean-shaven individual, his dark, curly hair slickered and shining. Rings glinted on the slim fingers of both hands and he was clad in a pale-blue suit and ruffle-fronted white silk shirt.

There was a smile on his lean, handsome face as he studied Ethan.

Ethan changed direction and took up a position before the seated man.

'Lucky Calhoun. The last time I saw you was when I ran you outa Sioux City three years ago. You still relieving the gullible of their hard-earned pay?'

Lucky's smiled broadened.

'Still got your sense of humour eh, Ethan? I'd heard that you had retired?'

'Tried to, but it didn't work out. You work here now or just passing through?'

'My passing-through days are over. I own this place. Sit down, Ethan, have a coffee or something stronger an' we can jaw over the old times.'

'I'll pass that one up, Lucky, but I reckon we'll be talking again real soon about present times an' future times.'

'Any time, Ethan,' Lucky responded. 'But then you might have your hands too full to worry 'bout me.'

'You think so?'

'I heard what you did to Floyd Tupper an' that's gonna cause his boss, Jackson Quinn, a whole heap o' grief. He likes things run his way. Quinn's a hard man an' runs a hard crew an' he'll be looking for a scalp to hang on his belt.'

'I'll be sure to keep my hat on,' Ethan replied dryly. He left the saloon hearing Lucky chuckle after him.

'I do like a man with a sense of humour. I'll get 'em to write it on your tombstone!'

Ethan smiled to himself. There was no love lost between the two men. Beneath the genial façade Lucky presented to the world, lurked a far more scheming, dangerous man.

Ethan reached the far end of town, crossed over and returned on the other side of the street. The buildings were mostly of clapboard, only the bank boasting stone walls.

He counted two brothels and a second, smaller saloon called The Cowman.

There were a few groups of drifters lounging about and he felt their hostility as he passed them by, but so far none had been boozed up enough to challenge him.

Finally, returning to his office, he was greeted by the rich aroma of strong coffee issuing from a a coffee pot he had set to simmer on an old potbelly stove before he had set out on his rounds.

It was a little after noon that the daytime peace of Greenwood was disturbed by the thunder of hooves as Jackson Quinn and his band of men galloped into town and reined to a halt before the sheriff's office forming a loose half-circle behind Quinn. Even before the dust kicked up by the horses had settled, Jackson Quinn bawled out, 'Hey, you, in the sheriff's office, step outside now. We got business to talk over.'

For a moment nothing happened, then the partially open door of the office opened fully and Ethan stepped out. He carried a shotgun under his left arm.

'The name's Sheriff E. J. Hawkesbury,' Ethan supplied mildly, pausing at the edge of the raised sidewalk.

'You ain't no sheriff in my town, mister,' Quinn stated bluntly. 'I'm a reasonable man: you got five minutes to get outa town or you become a permanent resident in the town cemetery!'

5

For a long moment Ethan studied the grim, set face of the man before him.

'You must be Jackson Quinn of the Circle Q.'

Jackson Quinn curled a lip.

'I see you've heard o' me,' he said with some satisfaction. 'Then you must'a heard I'm a man o' my word an' mean what I say?'

'Them's mighty serious words, Mr Quinn. Threatening a serving peace officer recognized in five states, including Montana, could earn you a one to five prison sentence.'

'Well, you ain't recognized here,' Quinn countered belligerently. 'We got duly elected law in the shape of Floyd Tupper. You might be some hotshot lawman down south, but you ain't needed here.'

'I don' recall Tupper being elected.'

Doc had arrived as the townsfolk gathered to witness the confrontation between the two. It was he who spoke up, earning himself a glare from Quinn.

'I elected him,' Quinn shot back at Doc.

'Then, as a member of the Greenwood Town Council, I'm electing Mr Hawkesbury as the new sheriff of Greenwood.'

'Keep outa this, Doc,' Quinn warned.

'I have for too long. Decent folk are quitting town because it ain't safe to walk the streets at night.'

'I stand with Doc.' The lanky, balding form of Abner Grange, proprietor of the general store, pushed through the crowd to join ranks with Doc who had planted himself beside Ethan. 'I'm losing money 'cause I have to shut up early. With so many saddle bums and drifters in town, I ain't staying open to be robbed. Tupper hightails it out o' town at sunset leaving us wi'out protection. Mr Hawkesbury's got my vote.'

There was a general murmur and nodding of heads from the gathered crowd that was not lost on Quinn.

'That's two votes to your one, Quinn. E.J stays,' Doc declared triumphantly.

Quinn fixed Ethan with a baleful stare.

'Could be you've made the biggest mistake of your life, mister,' he grated out harshly.

'No, you did, Quinn,' Ethan returned stonily. 'The day you sent Link Teal and his saddle trash to beat up a horse rancher on High Ridge, burn his home and steal his horses and leave him for dead.'

'The man was trespassing. That land is mine an' I protect my land the way I see fit.'

'Not according to the land office in Billings.'

'Well, they're wrong; the land is mine!' Quinn repeated. 'Anyway, what's that fella to you?'

'That fella was me, Quinn,' Ethan replied softly, eyes flashing. 'I changed my name to Hawk, figured I could retire from peace-keeping an' raise horses instead. It was working out real fine until your boys turned up, destroyed everything I owned an' damn near destroyed me.' A wintry smile tugged at his bearded lips. 'You took away my future, Quinn, an' now all I've got left is my past.' Ethan stopped and turned his head at the sound of hoofbeats.

From the southern end of town a group of riders appeared. As they grew nearer, their leader, a man in a tan jacket and blue Levis, called them to a halt. He himself rode forward, through Quinn's half-circle of men and drew his bay mare to a halt at right-angles to Quinn. Both men eyed each other.

'What the hell are you doing here, Brady?' Quinn was the first to break the silence.

'Same as you, Quinn, paying my respects to the new law I heard 'bout. That is what you are doing, ain't it, Jackson, paying your respects?' The newcomer didn't wait for an answer, but turned hie weathered face towards Ethan. 'Name's Bob Brady of the Boxed B, Sheriff. Thought you might need some support, moral or otherwise.'

'That's real neighbourly of you, Mr Brady, but Mr Quinn was just about to leave. Ain't that so, Mr Quinn?'

'Have your day while you can, mister, it ain't likely to last long,' Jackson Quinn snarled back.

'I'll bear that in mind. By the way, one other point: I gotta good memory for names an' faces. Seem to recollect a cattle thief by the name of Floyd Tupper down Texas way, three years back. He ran an active little band of rustlers until one night he ran into more'n he bargained for. His men were killed, but he got away.' Ethan slipped his gaze on to a white-faced Floyd Tupper as he spoke. 'Seem to remember there was a dodger put out on him by the Texas Rangers. Guess I'll have to get me a copy.'

Tupper squirmed beneath Ethan's gaze, but said nothing.

With a final glare at Ethan, Quinn turned his mount and cantered away. Tupper followed with Quinn's men falling in behind.

Bob Brady smiled cheerfully at Quinn's retreating back.

'It's been a long time since someone bested Quinn.' His face grew serious. 'The last man to do that was the sheriff afore Tupper an' he ended up dead.'

'Occupational hazard,' Ethan replied lightly.

'If'n you need help anytime, you can count on the Boxed B,' Bob Brady offered.

'I'll bear it in mind, Mr Brady.'

'Bob, Sheriff. My pa was Mr Brady. Good luck! Doc. Abner, got me some business for you.'

'Right away, Bob. See you Sheriff.'

Abner darted away as Bob Brady wheeled his horse about. The crowd that had gathered had rapidly dispersed leaving only Ethan and Doc Blanchard on the sidewalk.

'Coffee's brewed,' Ethan directed at Doc and the other nodded.

'Sounds fine to me,' Doc replied, and followed Ethan back into the sheriff's office.

★　★　★

'Cattle rustler, a damn, low-life cattle rustler. Get outa my sight, Tupper, I'll deal with you later.'

Sam Quinn had never seen his father in such a rage before as from his position on the shady veranda before the ranch house he watched as Jackson Quinn berated the luckless Tupper who stood cowed and silent in front of the older man before scurrying away.

'Trouble, Pa?' Sam asked, as the old man stormed on to the veranda.

'Nothin' I can't handle,' Quinn snapped back, and stomped into the house. Sam thought of following him then shrugged off the idea. Later perhaps, when the old man had cooled off. In the meantime, when Benson came back, he'd send the man to the bunkhouse to find out what happened in town.

Alone in his study, Jackson Quinn poured himself a big whiskey. Everything had gone wrong and he had ended up looking the fool. He had not expected such a show of support for the upstart stranger who had installed himself as sheriff, support that had been started by Doc Blanchard and Abner Grange. Well, they could be and would be taken care of.

He swallowed the whiskey in a single gulp, hardly noticing the fiery burn at the back of his throat and poured himself another and let a thin, vicious smile tug at his lips. Let the new sheriff have his moment of glory. Come nightfall, when the hands went into town, Hawkesbury would find he had bitten off more than he could chew. By dawn they would be burying the new sheriff and then the townsfolk would be taught a lesson they would never forget.

The thought cheered him up some-what, after all Hawkesbury was one man. Against thirty or more of his roughest hands he would not stand a chance. Maybe he'd sweeten the pot a little with a thousand-dollar bonus going to the man who suceeded in plucking the feathers of the Hawk!

★   ★   ★

As Ethan poured coffee for him and Doc, the latter eyed him curiously.

'You don't beat about the bush do you, Ethan? You threw down the glove to Quinn an' he's gotta whole passel of mean rannies who'd be only too pleased to take it up. Seems to me that ain't the smartest way to start.'

Ethan smiled as he spooned sugar into the cups of black coffee and passed one to Doc.

'We all have our methods, Doc. I leave subtle to the lawyers an' politicians. I like to poke an' prod, rile 'em up a little an' see what happens.'

'A bullet in the back more'n likely,' Doc replied, with heavy pessimism. 'You need back-up, Ethan.'

'You worry too much, Doc,' Ethan jibed, as he sipped the strong, black coffee, appreciating the acrid bite of the liquid.

Doc shook his head mournfully.

'Ol' Mort Haynes, the sheriff afore Tupper, was of a like mind.' Doc sniffed and rubbed the end of his nose. 'He made good coffee too.'

Ethan's eyes narrowed on the doctor.

'You saying Quinn had somethin' to do with it, Doc?'

Doc Blanchard smiled bleakly.

'Ain't saying nothin' o' the such, Ethan. Quinn's a hard man an' there was no love lost 'tween the pair o' 'em, but I don' figure Quinn for a bush-whacker.'

'Did they find out who killed Haynes?'

Doc shook his head.

'A sheriff an' a coupla deputies came up from Billings an' poked around for a while, but in the end they figured that whoever it was, was long gone. They gave up after a couple weeks an' went home.' Doc shrugged. 'Guess we'll never know who or why.'

'I'll bear it in mind.'

'Well don' be too hard on Jackson. Was a time when he was a likeable man. Him an' his brother Seb built up the ranch.'

'Brother?' Ethan's eyebrows lifted. 'You never told me there were two of 'em.'

'Was,' Doc replied. 'Seb Jackson an' Cora, Jackson's wife, until one day Seb an' Cora lit out an' left Jackson with a five-year-ol' son to raise. That was twenty years ago. After that Jackson Quinn changed. He's practically a recluse on that ranch of his. Today was the first time he's been in town for two months. With his crew of hard men he rules Crow County an' the town from the ranch.'

'What happened to Seb an' Cora?'

'Went East, so I heard. Them running

off together hit Jackson hard. It still riles him, I guess, an' the mere mention of Seb or Cora's name is enough to throw him into a rage. That's why he's like he is now. So much hate wi' no release twists him up a little more each year. Was a time he cared 'bout the town, now . . . ' — Doc shrugged — 'it's a home for any owlhoot or drifter looking for a place to hide from the law.' Doc gave a bitter laugh. 'It works out jus' right for Quinn. These men come into town, mostly without a dime to their name, an' Quinn hires them, real cheap, to work at the ranch.'

'I've seen the same sort of set-up afore,' Ethan said with a nod. 'An' they get protection from the law by a tame lawman such as Tupper.'

'I see you get the picture,' Doc said, tossing back the last of his coffee and climbing to his feet. 'At least you'll be going into this mess wi' your eyes open.'

'Why do you stay, Doc?' Ethan asked.

'Someone's gotta patch up the

innocent, or mebbe I'm too old an' ornery to move on. Damned if'n I know, Ethan.' Doc moved to the door, paused and looked back at the big lawman with a sorrowful shake of his head. 'Could be the shortest term of office of any lawman. Get yoursel' some backup, Ethan. One man can't take on a town.'

'I don't intend to, Doc, just a saloon,' Ethan replied. 'Drop by for coffee tomorrow.'

Doc shook his head in amazement, raised a hand in a wave and stepped out onto the sidewalk.

★ ★ ★

As the mellow shadows of dusk thickened into the hard blackness of night a tension gripped Greenwood that was matched only by the change in the weather.

Clouds had been building up over the distant hills to the north and now, as night advanced, lightning flickered over the far off rimrock and the faint echo of thunder pierced the humid, sultry night.

Men crowded into the Silver Wheel saloon, curious to see what this new sheriff would do. They had been arriving since dusk, now as eleven o'clock approached, they still waited in nervous anticipation for the Hawk to appear. Nothing had been seen of him so while they waited they drank, hiding their nervousness behind cheap, gutrot whiskey and loud laughter.

Apart from the bright wedge of light that fanned out from the Silver Wheel, the rest of the town was in darkness.

Ethan, clad in a long, grey duster, a shotgun cradled in his arms, moved along the darkened sidewalk towards the oasis of light. He moved with a slow, unhurried tread, booted feet echoing hollowly on the weathered, creaking boards. His eyes were never still as he walked, searching every shadow for any movement, ears tuned to pick up any stealthy sound that might mean a waiting bushwhacker.

The discordant jangle of a piano grew louder as he drew closer overlaid with increasingly raucous laughter and screams of delight from the saloon girls.

A grim smile played on Ethan's bearded lips as the rush of adrenalin surged through him, heightening his senses as he prepared to face the unknown.

Figures moved on the sidewalk outside the saloon; drunken cowboys, some hardly able to stand, laughing and calling out between themselves or shouting back through the batwings for a friend. One was throwing up noisily while another urinated into the road.

It was into this group that Ethan stepped.

Eyes focused with difficulty on the new arrival and from one of the drunks Ethan heard a startled, 'It's him!'

'Got me a mind to earn mysel' that thousand dollars,' a dark figure declared, words slurred as he started to peel away from the wall only to be pulled back by his companion.

'Don' be a goddam fool!' his saviour said harshly.

Figures staggered from his path. Ethan paid them only the briefest attention before passing through the batwings into the saloon. He had heard the drunkard's words. Doc had been right a price had been put on his head and that was going to make things a whole heap more interesting.

The air inside was thick with smoke from cigar and quirly that momentarily itched and prickled Ethan's eyes. He began to push his way, none too gently, through the drinkers. They turned, cursing, ready to challenge, only to fall back into silence beneath Ethan's gaze. Even though many had not seen him before they knew instinctively that this was the man everyone was talking about.

For those seeking confirmation, beneath the open duster a sheriff's star gleamed brightly from a dark lapel.

Saloon girls lined the rail of the

balcony that ran the length of the saloon above the long counter. They called down lewd and indecent suggestions to the sea of heads below.

Ethan reached the near corner of the counter, hefted the shotgun and, pointing it to the smoke-hazed ceiling, pulled the trigger.

The roar of the gun and belch of cordite smoke had the men closest to Ethan scattering in all directions to leave him standing in his own space. The girls above screamed and ran for the safety of the rooms that backed the balcony. Heads turned in the direction of the shot, conversation dropping off. Even the yellow-vested piano player came to an abrupt halt, sweating face craned around.

'The name's E.J. Hawkesbury, Sheriff of Crow County, an' if'n anyone's gotta problem with that, then speak out now.' Ethan challenged, as he broke open the shotgun and slid a round of heavy buckshot into the smoking breech and slammed it shut.

Lucky Calhoun pushed himself through the silent men and faced Ethan, a sorrowful smile on his handsome face.

'Dammit, Ethan, you ain't got no cause to go shooting that thing off in here,' he complained.

Ethan gave the slim, dapperly dressed man a cold eye.

'This place is closed for the night. Shut it down an' clear everyone out, Calhoun.'

'Now hold on a minute, Ethan,' Calhoun began.

'The name's Sheriff E. J. Hawkesbury,' he cut in sharply.

'You can't close me down, Sheriff, ain't no one causing any trouble here,' Calhoun objected and the gathered crowd, recovered from the initial shock, nodded their heads and growled their agreement, eyes hostile on Ethan.

'Men spewing an' pissing in the street outside ain't a good image for a family town. Now clear this saloon, Calhoun.'

Lucky Calhoun gave Ethan a hard, vicious smile.

'You do it, Sheriff, if'n you can.' He moved back and disappeared into the crowd leaving Ethan surrounded by a sea of angry, hostile men whose confidence was returning with every passing second.

Jesse Monk, standing at the counter, a foot resting on the brass foot-rail, raised a glass to his lips and dashed its contents into his mouth.

'Heard you ain't the proper sheriff here, mister,' he grunted, banging the glass down on to the polished top. 'Fill it up, barkeep,' he cried, not looking at Ethan.

Ethan surveyed the brutish, bearded profile. He had a good memory for faces and this one struck a chord.

Jesse Monk. A bully of a man and a tolerably fast draw. He dredged out what he could recall of the man as the fat barkeep nervously filled the waiting glass and then scurried away.

Monk was a real hard man. He had

been associated with a number of crimes from murder to robbery, but with no real evidence to ever convict him. He also recalled that Monk had a partner; a little runt of a man called Amos Stokes and where one was the other was not far away. It troubled Ethan that Stokes was nowhere to be seen. From what he could remember of the way the two worked, Monk prodded and riled from the front while Stokes came in silently from behind.

'What else have you heard?' Ethan enquired blandly.

'Heard that you had retired. Mebbe you should have stayed that way.

'An' mebbe you should have stayed in Arizona, Monk.'

Monk snapped his head around in surprise.

'You know me?'

'Know of you, an' none of it's good.'

Monk smirked, downed his waiting drink and stepped away from the counter and faced Ethan, hands dropping to the buckle of his gunbelt where they stayed, thumbs hooked behind.

'Guess it's time we found out just how good the Buscadero really is,' Monk suggested.'

Behind the two men customers dived out of the line of fire.

6

As the customers scattered, Ethan glimpsed movement at the edge of his vision; a dark, crouching figure had appeared on the balcony above, hunkered down, the barrel of a Winchester poked between the wooden rails.

'You're all washed up, Sheriff, now you're a dead man,' Monk taunted and went for his guns.

What happened next was the stuff of which legends are made. To those in the saloon it was something that would be talked about for a long time.

The shotgun was in Ethan's left hand, stock resting on his hip, barrel pointing upwards. As Monk made his play the shotgun roared and at the same time, Ethan, his eyes on Monk, went for the Adams holstered at his side.

The wooden rails before Amos

Stokes's crouching form flew apart in a shower of splinters. The heavy calibre rounds of shot punched into Stokes's upper body shattering ribs and shredding the flesh of his lower face in a gory explosion of blood and bone fragments. The man was lifted up and thrown backwards, the rifle flying from his hands. He hit the back wall and was sliding down when Ethan's pistol cleared leather and two bullets ploughed into Monk's body sending the man spinning in a staggering death twirl.

Monk had been fast, but Ethan had been a fraction faster, the double-action weapon pumping out two shots even as Monk's finger tightened on the trigger of his own weapon.

His finger spasmed. The Colt roared and a bullet punched a hole in the boards between Ethan's feet.

Monk was dead before he hit the floor. On the balcony, a split second later, Stokes's body toppled sideways and lay still.

Taking advantage of the shocked disbelief that gripped the crowded bar-room Ethan reholstered his pistol and smoothly reloaded the shotgun, this time lowering it to point forward and he turned slowly on his heels, the barrel of the shotgun sweeping over the gathered men in a deadly arc, causing them to flinch backwards as the barrel passed.

'If'n anyone else has a mind to take up where Monk left off, then step up, don' be shy,' he invited, but there were no takers. Ethan allowed himself a cold smile as his eyes raked the silent crowd. 'I've heard it said that I'm worth a thousand dollars, dead. I guess Monk thought it was easy money. A lot of hard-nosed rannies have tried over the years.' He paused, looking around. 'Well I'm still alive, they ain't.'

He turned until he faced back down the long room. At the far end, a few yards from where the piano player sat, stood a big, gaudy faro wheel. Ethan took the shotgun now in both hands, but still kept it at waist level.

'I'd advise you gents to move,' he said quietly.

Men dived for cover overturning tables in their haste as the shotgun roared.

The faro wheel flew apart.

'I ain't agin gambling, I ain't agin drinking an' I ain't agin saloon girls.' Ethan spoke up as he reloaded the shotgun. 'Man's gotta take time out to enjoy himsel' after a day's hard work. But when that enjoyment makes decent folk hide themselves away, scared to come out after dark, then it makes me kinda fretful.' He swung the shotgun in the direction of the piano.

The yellow-vested piano player's eyes popped. He gave a screech and hit the floor. The shotgun blasted and the front of the piano splintered. Strings snapped in a discordant chord of destruction as the keys shattered into ivory splinters.

'The Silver Wheel is closed for the night an' will be closed every night at this time. You men git to your homes an' if'n I find anyone about when I step outside you'll spend the night in jail. I've seen a lotta faces here that look real familiar. I'll be going through a pile of dodgers in the next coupla days, an' if'n those faces are still around . . . ' He didn't need to complete the sentence, the meaning was all too clear.

There was a noisy clamour to clear the saloon and a few minutes later Ethan found himself alone with only the barkeep and Lucky Calhoun for company.

Calhoun faced Ethan, an angry flush to his face.

'You had no call to shoot up my place, Hawkesbury,' he said sullenly. 'I've gotta living to make, too.'

'You had your chance, Calhoun, now I'm calling the tune.'

He started to brush past the saloon owner and Calhoun caught his arm.

'What about them?' He indicated the dead bodies of Monk and Stokes.

Ethan shook off the man's hand.

'Think what you would have done

had it been me lying there an' do the same for them,' Ethan replied, and headed for the batwings.

Calhoun glared after him. 'You might have won tonight, Sheriff, but there are a lotta 'tonights' yet to come,' he called out.

Ethan turned at the batwings. 'I'll bear it in mind, Calhoun,' he replied, turned and slipped out into the night.

Lightning still played over the distant peaks and the faint rumble of thunder touched his ears as he made a round of the town.

Word had preceded him. Greenwood's other saloon, The Cowman, smaller and much less grand than the Silver Wheel, was empty as he passed by, but he felt obliged to enter.

Seth Wilkins, owner and barkeep, paused in swamping the floor.

'Heard what happened at the Silver Wheel, Sheriff, so did my customers.' Then in a surprising move he offered a hand to Ethan. 'Wilkins, Seth Wilkins, Sheriff.' Seth smiled. He was a big man with an easy, crooked smile, his broad face topped with a mass of dark curly hair, but when he moved it was with a pronounced limp in his right leg. 'I'd offer you a drink, but in the present circumstances . . . ' he continued as Ethan took the strong hand.

'Some other time, Mr Wilkins.'

'Whenever, Sheriff, an' I'd be obliged you call me Seth.'

'Nice meeting you, Seth.' Ethan obliged with a smile, still surprised at the man's apparent friendliness, but at the same time suspicious.

The two talked for a moment then Ethan left and continued his rounds still puzzled by the man's show of friendliness.

By dawn, the promised storm in the north had not materialized. Ethan watched the sun come up with tired eyes. He had had little sleep during an uneventful night following the incident in the Silver Wheel. The town had remained quiet save for the squeak and rattle of the undertaker's cart as he was rousted out of bed to remove the bodies of Monk and Stokes from the saloon.

The town was rousing itself as Ethan made himself a pot of strong coffee to start the day. Later on he would take a bath and hopefully get some sleep.

He whirled as the door of the office opened, hand closing over the butt of the Adams, but he relaxed as he saw the girl standing there.

Laura Treece swallowed and smiled nervously at him.

'Morning, Sheriff. My name's Laura Treece, I own the café down the street.'

Ethan nodded and smiled. 'I remember, ma'am.'

'Then I'd be obliged if'n you'd take breakfast with me. That's if'n you've a mind to. It'll be on the house. A kind of welcoming breakfast.'

'That's real nice o' you, ma'am. I'd surely like that. Give me a few moments to wash up an' I'll be over.'

She smiled prettily.

'Fifteen minutes an' it'll be on the table.'

'I'll be there, ma'am,' he promised.

'Laura, Sheriff, Laura,' she said, turned and left the office.

He was there in ten and the plate of steak and potatoes topped with three eggs that was placed before him made his mouth water.

'I hope it's to your liking, Sheriff. There'll be coffee to follow,' Laura said.

'Ain't seen a finer sight in a coon's age,' Ethan declared. 'Thank you, ma'am . . . Laura. Folks call me a lot of different names, but my given one is Ethan.'

She blushed. 'I'll leave you to eat, Ethan. See to my other customers.'

'Don' you worry 'bout me.' Ethan picked up his knife and fork. 'I'm gonna be kinda' busy myself for a spell.'

Ethan, hunger assuaged, was on his second cup of coffee when Doc appeared and made straight for him.

'I hear I missed all the excitement last night.' He pulled a chair from another table and flopped down facing Ethan, a wry expression on his

106

face. 'I declare, Ethan, you are a surprising man.'

'None more than to mysel', Doc.'

'The whole town's buzzing wi' what you done last night.'

'Coffee, Doc?' Laura appeared.

'Good an' strong, Laura. I may not have been saving the world last night, but I was sure bringing another citizen into it.'

'Mary's had her baby?' Laura asked.

'Boy. Eight pounds of pure, yelling noise. Mother an' baby both doing fine.' Doc sniffed. 'That's the seventh one. I sure wish Wilbur would curb his desires for a spell.'

'Hush now, Doc. It gets lonely out there and ain't much to do when it gets dark,' Laura defended with a smile.

'Well, if'n Wilbur keeps it up, it ain't gonna stay lonely for long.' Doc shook his head and Laura moved away laughing. Doc eyed Ethan reflectively. 'So, how does a man shoot a pair of killers coming at him from two different directions at the same time an' live to tell the tale?'

Ethan smiled briefly. 'You don' need to aim with a shotgun, Doc, jus' pull the trigger,' Ethan replied with a shrug.

Doc shook his head. 'Damn, wish I'd been there.'

Laura appeared with Doc's coffee as the café began to fill up.

'I met Seth Wilkins last night. Seemed a friendly sort o' character in spite of everything.'

'Seth, he's one of the best. Used to be a puncher for Frank Brady till he busted his leg pretty bad an' couldn't sit a horse no more. It was then he took over The Cowman from old Pete Trescot, must be ten, eleven years ago now. In them days The Cowman was the only saloon in Greenwood an' still is for my money. Seth serves up a decent drink at a fair price.'

'How long's Calhoun an' the Silver Wheel been here?'

'Year or so now. He bought up a couple stores an' had them converted into the Silver Wheel. That, an'

Tupper's ineffectual law-keeping drew the riff-raff from far an' wide. Made Greenwood an open town for the lawless.'

Ethan frowned. 'Seems to me that Quinn still holds the reins around here, so what does he get from letting the town run wild?'

'Cheap labour, I guess. Most of the rannies that drift into town are on the run from somewhere. He hires them for less than the going rate an' offers protection from the law for as long as they work for him. It's worked out pretty good for him up till now, so I guess he ain't gonna be too happy that you're still around this morning.' Doc grinned. 'Reckon he'll be fit to bust when he hears.' Doc chuckled, shaking his head, then his expression grew serious as he studied Ethan. 'You look tired. You need to rest,' he advised soberly.

Ethan smiled wanly. 'Guess that's a luxury I can't afford jus' now.'

'You need a deputy. Someone to spell

you while you sleep. Tiredness takes the edge off a man,' Doc warned.

'Ain't too many looking for that kinda job in Greenwood. I'll make out, Doc, I've been here afore.'

* * *

Jackson Quinn was more than fit to bust and his mood was not helped by the tall form of Lucky Calhoun helping himself to his whiskey as though he owned the place. It was mid-morning and all Quinn had heard about around the ranch was the events of the previous evening in the Silver Wheel saloon. Six men had already quit; now, Calhoun was here whining his loss.

'So what are you gonna do about Hawkesbury?' Calhoun asked, as he returned to the desk where Quinn was seated and sprawled himself in the facing chair. 'He busted up my saloon real good. Gonna takes weeks to replace the wheel an' piano an' by the looks o' my customers, half ain't gonna return while he's about.'

'That's your problem,' Quinn grated back.

'Look,' Calhoun objected. 'I put a lot of my own money in the Silver Wheel. We had an arrangement. I found the men to work for you; in return you let Geenwood become an open town. Well Hawkesbury's closed it down an' that's bad for my business. I seen him work on a town afore an' he don't stop till it's squeaky clean.' Calhoun tossed back the whiskey in a single swallow. 'An' that ain't only the drifters an' saddle tramps. I seen him take out corrupt judges an' big ranchers. He ain't a bit fussy who he goes up agin, high or low.'

'So what do you expect me to do?' Quinn shot back.

'Protect your investment. As a silent, invisible partner you were getting a good weekly return on your money. That ain't gonna happen no more with Hawkesbury around.'

'If'n he can't be killed then we get him on the payroll. Ain't a man I know who can't be bought.'

Quinn's statement caused Calhoun to vent a hoot of derisive laughter.

'Then you don't know Hawkesbury. Man tried that once. Big rancher down Sonora way. He had the same idea. He died with twenty thousand dollars still in his hand that he was trying to give to Hawkesbury. The man ain't interested in money, jus' the law.'

Quinn glared at Calhoun, hating the man's defeatist attitude.

'Dammit, Calhoun, the man's human. If'n he eats enough lead then he'll die.'

'The problem is in getting the lead into him,' Calhoun responded.

'Leave it to me, Calhoun. Jus' get that saloon up an' running for business.'

Calhoun deposited the empty glass on the edge of the desk after climbing to his feet, a smile on his face.

'I'll be in touch.'

Jackson Quinn watched the man depart. He didn't like Calhoun, but business was business and where money was concerned he put aside his feelings.

★　★　★

They had the dog cornered in an alley that ran between the bank and the grain store. Drawn there by a group of yelling youngsters prodding at it with sticks, Ethan observed the animal cowering back in a deep doorway recessed in the side wall of the grain store.

It wasn't much of a mutt, its lean, black hide matted with dust and burcs. It pressed itself into a corner, hunkered down on its hind quarters, one front paw held up, a token snarl exposing sharp teeth.

One youth, older than the rest, gripped a hay fork and was being urged on by the others to 'stick' the dog.

'Git him, Jake. Use the fork,' one youngster, no more than ten years old urged.

Jake stood undecided, gripping the fork tightly as he pointed the double prongs at the animal.

He was a lanky youth clad in ragged clothes, straw-coloured hair poking from beneath the brim of a floppy hat. He looked to be in his late teens.

No one saw Ethan approach, all eyes on the silver prongs that they expected any moment to be turned red by the dog's blood.

'Go on, Jake. Ol' man Quinn's offered twenty dollars for his hide,' another voice prompted.

'I'm a'gonna, I'm a'gonna,' Jake cut back hoarsely, but still holding back. Somehow he didn't have the heart to kill the defenceless animal, but he had got himself into the situation that if he did not go through with it, he'd be branded yellow by the rest of the boys.

He prayed for some miracle to get him out of the present situation and save face at the same time.

'What in tarnation's going on here?' Ethan's voice roared out making the boys jump and throw aside their sticks.

Jake almost cried out in relief as he dropped the hay fork and faced Ethan. 'Well?' Ethan demanded sternly.

'Nothin', Sheriff,' Jake muttered.

'I heard mention of twenty dollars for his hide. Who's paying? Speak up, boy. I ain't a patient man, so don't rile me.'

Jake swallowed, terror gripping him.

'Ol' dog's been causing trouble at the Circle Q. Mr Quinn said he'd pay for someone to get rid of it.'

Ethan's eyes travelled from boy to boy and they cringed back from the tall, bearded nemesis looming over them.

'You boys should be in school. Make sure you're there when I come by later,' he barked. 'Now git afore I change my mind an' throw you all in jail.'

They needed no second bidding. There was a stampede of feet as the group fled leaving Jake on his own.

'You gonna shoot me, Sheriff?' Jake asked, quaking in his boots.

Ethan glared at him.

'I damn well ought to, boy. I don't take kindly to animals being mistreated, but I must be feeling kind today. What's your name, boy?'

'Jake, sir, Jake Tolliver.'

'An' what do you do when you're not mistreating dumb animals?'

'I work at the livery with Mr Rusty,' Jake replied.

Ethan rolled his eyes.

'Then, Jake Tolliver, get your sorry hide outa here an' take that thing with you.' Ethan indicated the hay fork. 'Just remember, I'll be keeping my eye on you in the future.'

'Yes, sir!' Jake didn't need to be told twice. Grabbing up the hayfork he ran from the alley.

'Mind what you do wi' that thing; like as not you'll stick some innocent citizen an' then I'll have to throw you in jail,' he bellowed at Jake's retreating back.

Ethan smiled ruefully as he turned back to the dog only to find that it, too, had seized its chance to escape. Ethan caught sight of it at the far end of the alley that opened on to the warren of back-lots that ran behind the town. It was limping badly on its left, front forepaw.

Ethan blew noisily through his lips and shrugged his bearded cheeks.

'Good luck, fella,' he called softly in its wake, before turning and heading back into the town. He hoped he had frightened them enough to keep them out of mischief for a while.

7

Ethan continued his round of the town without further incident, returning an hour later, tired and weary, to his office. Here he discarded hat and jacket and eased himself into the seat behind the desk, glad to be off his feet. He massaged the back of his neck with one hand and allowed himself to relax.

He must have allowed himself to relax too much, for suddenly he found himself jerking awake, unaware that he had fallen asleep for a few minutes, hand reaching automatically for the holstered Adams.

A noise, something, had awoken him.

The front door that had been partially open was now wide open and something he couldn't see, only hear, was moving on the other side below the height of the desk.

Nerves taut as he came awake, he

jerked to his feet fisting the Adams as the dog, still limping badly, came into sight.

'Jesus H, dog, you come near to getting your ugly head blowed off,' Ethan said with relief in his voice, as he reholstered the Adams.

The dog reached the pot-bellied stove and settled itself down, looking with dark, bright eyes at Ethan, its pink tongue lolling from the side of its mouth.

Ethan moved from behind the desk and hunkered down in front of the animal.

'You look like you're carrying some trouble there, fella,' he murmured. The dog rolled on to its side and obligingly lifted its troubled paw. 'How 'bout I take a look, eh?' Ethan took the paw and saw immediately what the trouble was. Between the fleshy pads of the paw he could see the end of a thorn protruding. 'Reckon this could hurt a mite, fella, but that's gotta come out.' He continued to talk to the animal as he gripped the end of the thorn between thumb and forefinger then with one quick movement he jerked the thorn out.

The dog gave a whimper and snatched his paw from Ethan's grip, rolling up on to its stomach.

Ethan rose to his feet and surveyed the inch-long thorn.

'That's one helluva piece o' timber to be toting about, fella.'

In response the dog thumped the wooden flooring once with its tail before commencing to lick the injured area.

Ethan stood looking down at it for awhile after dropping the thorn into the stove before rummaging around in his own belongings to produce an old army mess tin that he filled with water from a jug and put it down before the dog.

It came to its feet and stood awkwardly on three legs lapping noisily at the water.

By the time it had finished, Ethan had produced a wedge of jerky and tossed it to the dog.

'Ain't much, but it'll keep you going.'

The dog grabbed up the jerky and settled itself down by the stove again to eat it.

Ethan smiled down at the stray.

'So, what have you been up to to make Jackson Quinn put a price on your head, eh?' The dog looked up at Ethan and its tail thumped the boards in a single wag before it returned its attention to the piece of jerky. 'Guess that makes us pards. Ol' Quinn ain't too fond o' me either.'

Ethan crossed to the door and stepped out on to the sidewalk. The long, meandering Main Street shimmered in the hot afternoon sun. He looked both ways, but few people were about. Returning to the office, he paused only long enough to gather up his shotgun before heading for the rear cell block. In the doorway between office and cell block, he halted and looked back at the dog whose head and forepaws were just visible jutting out from behind the stove.

'Feel free to take yourself off if'n you've a mind to, but if'n you're staying I'd appreciate you didn't mess on the floor. Savvy?'

The dog stopped its chewing and peered around the side of the stove at Ethan, regarding the big man with its dark, intelligent eyes.

Ethan shook his head, still smiling. He figured that times were getting bad if all he could find to talk to was one mangy, scrawny, ugly piece of multiple cross-breeding.

He headed for the centre cell, stretched himself out on the hard bench and, using his bedroll as a pillow, fell asleep.

An hour later, he was jerked awake by a furious barking and the sound of a man's voice raised in alarm. He tumbled from the cell, shotgun at the ready, and charged into the outer office only to find Doc pressed against one wall, the dog bracing him and alternately barking and snarling.

'Git this damned hell-hound offa me,' Doc squawked as Ethan appeared.

Ethan snapped out a command and the dog fell silent, retreating to the side of the stove where it sat, eyes still fixed suspiciously on Doc.

Ethan grinned and patted the dog's head.

'Well, if'n that don't beat all. Well done, fella.'

The dog, sensing the approval in the big man's voice, lifted its head to push a wet muzzle into Ethan's hand and licked it.

'Is it safe to move?' Doc demanded.

'I ain't too sure, Doc. Come over an' git acquainted.'

Grumbling to himself, Doc moved cautiously to Ethan's side. The dog stopped its licking to watch the other, a snarl building in its throat.

Ethan tapped it on the nose sharply.

'He's a friend. Let him take a sniff o' your hand, Doc.'

'Dammit, Ethan, he might take my hand off.'

'No, I fed him earlier,' Ethan replied drolely.

With a certain amount of misgiving Doc reached out a hand. The dog sniffed it and then lay down.

'Coffee, Doc?'

Relieved that his hand was still attached to his arm, Doc nodded and retreated to a chair keeping a wary eye on the animal.

'Where'd he come from?' Doc asked.

'I was hoping you might be able to tell me.' Ethan launched into his tale of how he found the dog. 'Seems to have taken a shine to me since that moment. Any idea who the owner might be?'

'Was would be better. Thanks.' Doc took the coffee Ethan brought across to him.

'I'm not following you, Doc.'

'That's Blackie, he belonged to Sheriff Haynes. Used to go everywhere with him, then when Haynes got hissel' killed, ol' Blackie took off. He comes into town every once in a while, but mostly he stays away. How he's managed to survive, I ain't too sure. But that's where he always sat, alongside the stove. Looks like he's finally come home.'

'How come Jackson Quinn's offered a reward for his hide?'

Doc shrugged and pushed his hat back to scratch at his hairline.

'Beats me, Ethan. Story is that he's been seen worrying Circle Q beeves, but that ol' hound ain't a cattle worrier. Reckon me'sel' it's a link to Haynes that Jackson would like to get rid of once an' for all. Close the book on the ex-sheriff forever.'

Ethan dropped into his chair, tilted it back and swung his feet up on the desk, ankles crossed, nursing the mug of coffee on his lap.

'So, what was the story on Haynes an' Quinn? Happen you were gonna tell me.'

'Not much to tell really. The town council with the exception of Quinn elected Haynes to office. He didn't like Haynes because the man was apt to speak his mind.' He glared pointedly at Ethan. 'Jus' like someone else I could name. He wouldn't let himself be influenced by others.'

'A man after my own heart,' Ethan approved.

'I wouldn't say that.' Doc rubbed the tip of his nose. 'Mort Haynes used the law to his own advantage. If'n he saw a way of making money from it, he'd be there in the front of the queue with his hand out. One of his favourite tricks was to fine any man who ended up in his jail. He said it helped with the upkeep of the jail. Truth is the money went into his own pocket. Mind, I ain't saying he weren't a good lawman. He kept the town free of bums and drifters an' no man or woman was afraid of walking the streets at night. No, there was somethin' between the two of 'em.'

'How'd you mean?'

'For starters, Quinn's a hard man, he don't scare easy, but I swear he was afraid of Haynes. That's only my opinion, mind, but if'n it came to a difference of opinion between the two, Quinn was always the one to back down. It was as though Haynes had a hold over the man.'

'Interesting. Any idea what?'

'Nope. Haynes was here a little over six months afore he was found on the trail outside town beaten to death. Real nasty that. As far as I can make out the two had never met afore until Haynes came here. An' while he was here Haynes found something out 'bout Quinn that scared the ol' man. Haynes had extravagant tastes for a lawman an' had more money to spend than a sheriff earns.'

'So you figure Quinn was paying Haynes off to keep quiet about whatever?' Ethan suggested.

'Seems that way to me,' Doc agreed, placing his now empty mug on the edge of the desk. 'Though I don't know what.' Doc pulled a gold watch from a vest pocket as he spoke and frowned down at it. 'Tarnation, I gotta call out to the Charnwood place. Never knowed

Dan or his boys needing the attentions of a doctor afore.' With a sigh he rose to his feet eyes falling on Blackie before lifting to Ethan. 'Guess you gotta deputy now.'

'Happen I have,' Ethan agreed with a smile, unfolding his legs from the table. 'Take care, Doc.'

'That's all I do, take care of others, but who takes care of me? Answer me that then.'

'I reckon I best think on that for a spell,' Ethan said.

'You do that, an' if'n you ever come up with the answer, let me know for I ain't figured it yet.' Doc stomped across to the door and paused, looking back. 'An' make sure that hound don' savage some poor, innocent citizen.'

'He only bites outlaws,' Ethan replied with a grin.

Doc sniffed and left the office calling over his shoulder, 'They make up half the goddamn town!'

★　★　★

Ethan was keyed up by the time night fell. Those who wished him harm only came out after dark and there seemed to be a large number of horses hitched up outside the Silver Wheel.

He entered the saloon and the buzz of conversation slowly gave way to a hostile silence as he made his way to the bar through the smoke-hazed air. Sullen-eyed men stepped quickly aside to allow him passage to the bar.

'Dammit, Sheriff, you trying to kill my business off altogether?' Calhoun detached himself from a card game and followed Ethan belligerently. 'My customers are choosy who they drink with and right now you're putting them off their drink an' that ain't good for business.'

Ethan swung around to face the man, winter in his eyes.

'Don't push me, Calhoun or you'll be changing your name to 'Unlucky' Calhoun,' he warned darkly.

Calhoun hastily raised placatory

hands in a calming gesture.

'No need to get riled, Sheriff. You busted up my place pretty good, so I've a right to be upset an' being upset makes a man speak his piece.'

'You haven't seen 'busted' yet, Calhoun. I want this place cleared by the time I come back or I'll close it down completely, Hawkesbury style,' Ethan warned bleakly, turned away from the bar and strode out into the night.

Abner Grange was just closing the general store as Ethan emerged. The tall, lanky figure called Ethan across.

'Cain't remember the last time I closed up as late as this, Sheriff. Town's getting back to what it once was an' that feels good. Folks appreciate it.'

'My pleasure, Abner.' Ethan touched fingers to the brim of his hat and moved on into the night.

Others were less appreciative of him.

Big Mary stood in the doorway of the whorehouse she ran, bright golden light spilling from the doorway. She was very overweight and the generous proportions of her body were squeezed into a purple silk dress a size too small. She smoked a thin cigar and glared hostilely at Ethan as he came up.

'You're killing my business, Sheriff,' she rasped hoarsely from a tobacco-ruined throat.

Ethan paused briefly. 'The best advice I can offer you, ma'am, is to quit while you're still ahead. Look for another town. Pretty soon I'm gonna be closing you down. Evening, ma'am.' He moved off.

'Mebbe you should take your own advice, Sheriff,' she shrilled brokenly after him. 'Quit while you're ahead for it sure as hell ain't gonna last much longer!'

The darkness swallowed him up and he smiled grimly to himself. The town was as taut as a fiddle string and pretty soon it was going to snap. He hoped that he'd be ready for it when it happened.

The night passed quietly and he wondered sourly, as the dawn brightened the eastern horizon, how many more quiet nights there would be.

As the town woke up and main street began to bustle, Ethan breakfasted at Laura's and it was later, an empty plate before him, that the young man entered. He marched up to the counter tugging a black stetson from his head to reveal a mane of wavy blond hair and settled himself on a stool ordering a cup of coffee.

Ethan studied the youngster over his second cup of coffee.

He was tall and whipcord thin, his slim, square shoulders clad in a light tan buckskin jacket open over a light-blue shirt that matched the faded blue of his Levis. Ethan quickly noticed the Walker Colt slung low on his right hip and tied against his thigh with a leather cord. Boots that matched the hat in colour finished off the youngster's apparel.

Outside a lone, white-spotted calico

horse was carrying a saddle that he recognized as the type known as a California rig. A single centre cinch, high saddle horn and covered stirrups. Ethan hadn't seen one of those for a long while.

From the profile view he got, Ethan estimated the young man to be in his late teens, mebbe a little older, and exuding a confidence generally felt only by an older, wiser man.

As Laura poured the youngster his coffee he took this opportunity to glance around at the half a dozen or so customers. When he found himself under Ethan's stare, he nodded to the lawman and smiled.

'Morning, Sheriff,' he greeted.

'Howdy.' Ethan rose and moved to the counter to pay for his meal. 'Haven't seen a saddle rig like that for quite a spell.'

'Belonged to my pa, he died a while back. My name's Thaddeus Jones.' He smiled wryly and extended a hand. 'Mostly folks call me California.'

Ethan took the hand noting the other's strong grip.

'What brings you to Greenwood, California?'

'Jus' travelling, Sheriff, looking for a place to settle, mebbe.'

Ethan nodded at the youngster's guarded reply, but did not prompt him further.

'Enjoy your stay. Miss Laura.' He touched his hat brim to Laura.

'Bye, Ethan,' she called back as he headed for the door.

It turned out to be Ethan's day for meeting strangers. He had not been back in the office five minutes before the door opened. He looked up from leafing through a pile of dodgers expecting it to be Doc calling in for his morning coffee. Instead, a young man in a wheelchair was being pushed through the doorway by a huge mountain of a man, the latter ducking to avoid losing his hat on the lintel.

To Ethan's surprise, Blackie

scrambled to his feet, tail wagging at the entrance of the newcomer.

Sam Quinn smiled as the dog came across and stroked its head.

'Well, there you are, fella. Bin a long time, eh, but you sure don' forget.'

Blackie moved around to greet the big man and Sam rolled himself to the desk, leaned forward and extended a hand.

'Sam Quinn, Sheriff. I guess you've already met my pa.' He pulled a wry face.

Ethan stood up and leaned across the desk, shaking the firm hand that was offered.

'Not an easy man to get on with,' Ethan commented.

'Not an easy man to live with either,' Sam replied candidly. 'This 'ere's Pete Benson. He supplies the legs I ain't got. Without him I'd be chained to the ranch forever.'

'Pete,' Ethan acknowledged.

'Sheriff,' Pete returned.

'So what can I do for you, Mr

Quinn?' Ethan dropped back into his seat.

A pained expression crossed Sam's face.

'Call me Sam. I almost thought Pa had followed me in,' Sam laughed and Ethan found himself smiling. There was something eminently likeable about the young man, a quality totally lacking in his father. 'I have some business to do in town so I thought I'd drop by an' introduce mysel'. Pa has a tendency to ruffle feathers. It's his way. I try to smooth them out an' sometimes it's a hard chore.'

'From where I'm sitting you're doing a mighty fine job.'

'From what I've heard an' for what it's worth, I think you're jus' what this town needs, but I don' envy you the task ahead.'

'Mebbe you should try an convince your pa o' that.'

Before Sam could make a reply, there was a commotion from the doorway as

Abner Grange, the general store owner rushed in.

'Sheriff, you'd better come quick. Doc's horse has jus' come into town an' he ain't on it!'

8

Four riders left Greenwood, heading into the broken hill country that lay to the north-west and the Charnwood ranch that had been Doc's port of call the previous evening. Ethan led, with big Pete Benson, on a borrowed horse next to him. Behind, rode Abner Grange and the young stranger, California. Ahead loped Blackie. Somehow the urgency transmitted by Ethan had been picked up by the hound.

It wasn't much of a posse, but it was all Ethan could gather together at such short notice. Benson was there on the insistence of Sam Quinn.

'Take Pete, Sheriff, he knows the country better than most,' Sam had said and Pete was eager to be of assistance. Abner was there because he was a long-standing friend of the doc's, but California?

138

Ethan wasn't sure why he was here. The youngster was new in town. He had no reason to join in the hunt, but somehow he had attached himself to the party.

It was an hour's ride to the Charnwood ranch at a normal pace, but they did it in less, riding fast.

Dan Charnwood was splitting logs when the four rode up and he was quickly joined by his two sons, Seth and Ben. Dan, a widower of some six years, scratched his grizzled head.

'Doc? Ain't no one here sent for Doc, ain't that right, boys?'

'Sure, Pa,' Seth, the eldest boy agreed and Ben nodded, adding, 'Ain't no one ill here, Sheriff.'

'You sure he said he was coming here?' Dan questioned.

'Less'n there's more than one Charnwood place.'

'Only the one, Sheriff, an' this is it.'

Ethan felt a tightening of his stomach. Someone had deliberately sent the doc out on a false call and to his way of thinking that could only mean one thing.

'I'm obliged, gents, I reckon we've got some looking to do.'

'We'll come along,' Dan spoke up. 'Doc was good to my Annie whilst she was ailing. Boys, saddle us some horses.'

'I'm obliged again,' Ethan said.

'Say, what happened to Floyd Tupper. I thought he was sheriff of Greenwood?' Dan questioned, as Seth and Ben saddled three horses.

'Greenwood's under new management now,' Ethan replied grimly.

'An' there's some who don' like it much,' Abner cut in. ''Cause o' Ethan here I can keep my store open after dark agin. The town's coming back to the people.'

'Not afore time,' Dan said with a nod. He squinted up at Ethan. 'You must be some lawman to turn that town around.'

'I can vouch for that,' Abner cried. 'He's a famous man. Have you ever heard tell of the Buscadero?'

Dan's eyes popped and he stared anew at Ethan.

'Just doing my job,' Ethan said, feeling more than a little uncomfortable at Abner's enthusiastic introduction.

'Some job,' Dan breathed. 'Why I was in Big Butte when . . . '

Ethan was more than relieved when Seth and Ben appeared with the horses.

'Mount up, gents, an' let's be moving if'n we want to find Doc afore nightfall.' Ethan wheeled his horse about and headed off.

Three hours later, they found Doc in a brush-choked gully. No more would he pass the time of day drinking Ethan's coffee in the office.

He had died hard, beaten to a pulp, both arms broken and the fingers on one hand brutally splintered, the bones breaking through the flesh. His face had been mutilated by a series of savage blows before finally his neck had been broken to relieve the awful agony of those last terrible moments.

Ethan felt white-hot anger boil through him. Doc had not been a fighting man. He had spent his life relieving pain and for this to happen to him was a sacrilege.

No one said anything as they gently laid him across the horse Ben had been riding and tied him down for the journey back to Greenwood, but tears streaked Abner's mournful face.

'I'll make sure you get the horse back, Dan,' Ethan said, as they prepared to move out.

'Just you get whoever done that to Doc, Sheriff,' Dan replied hotly. 'An' if'n you need any help, me an the boys'll be ready.'

The two parties broke apart, Seth and Ben riding double as Dan led them back to the ranch while Ethan and the others headed back to Greenwood.

Ethan had very little doubts as to who had administered the brutal, murderous beating; the same men who had beat him near to death not so long ago: Link Teal and his rannies. The meeting between them was long over-due and it was something he was going to correct in the very near future and woebetide any man who stood in his way.

They worked for Jackson Quinn and if Quinn had ordered the death of Doc Blanchard then no power on earth would save the man from the gallows, no matter how rich or powerful he was or thought he was.

★　★　★

When Sam Quinn brought the news of Doc's death to his father, Jackson Quinn was visibly shocked. Later that afternoon, he saddled himself a bay mare and rode north-west towards the distant mountains.

'You damn fool, Teal, there was no need to kill Blanchard,' Quinn fumed, on reaching the distant line shack an hour after leaving the Circle Q.

The inside of the shack was hot and airless, heavy with the smell of cigarette smoke and the acrid bite of sweating, unwashed bodies.

At a central crude, wooden table, Teal, with Dawson, Roach and Stiles, sat and were playing cards when Quinn entered and delivered the angry outburst.

Teal scowled up at the intruder.

Chuck Dawson gave one of his toothy smiles and glanced slyly at Teal.

'That's the second time a Quinn has called you a fool, Link. Ain't a friendly way to speak to my mind,' he goaded.

Teal threw his cards on the table and leaned back in his chair, scowl deepening.

'I don' take to being called a fool, Mr Quinn.' He put emphasis on the *Mr* giving it an insulting slur.

Jackson Quinn's face reddened.

'While you take pay from me you'll take whatever I say or get out,' he challenged.

Dawson shook a hand as though he had just touched something hot.

'Lordy, I think the boss man is riled.'

'Too right I am. Hawkesbury knows you work for me and after what you did to him he's gonna put two an' two together. He's the kinda man who don' forget and with Blanchard dead he ain't about to forgive. Dammit, why'd you have to kill Blanchard?'

Teal grinned. 'I guess ol' Stiles got carried away. Takes his work real serious. Ain't that a fact, Stiles?'

Stiles, with his lank, black hair falling to his shoulders and big, calloused, bony hands, bobbed his head.

'Sure is, Link,' he admitted with a chuckle. The others were smiling, too, and Quinn felt a wave of revulsion wash through him. 'Didn't mean for to break his neck, it jus' happened.' There was almost a note of sorrow in his voice, sorrow that he had had his pleasure curtailed by Doc's untimely death.

'Pity you didn't do that to Hawkesbury when you had the chance,' Quinn snapped back and a sudden, cold smile tugged at his lips. 'Well, mebbe the next time you'll do it right.'

The smile left Teal's face.

'You want us to get rid of Hawkesbury for you? Well' it'll cost plenty.'

The smile stayed on Quinn's lips.

'Oh no, Teal, it ain't gonna cost me a dime. He's gonna come looking for you an' if'n you intend staying alive you'd better be ready because I don' reckon he'll be interested in taking prisoners.' Quinn's smile became a smirk as he glanced around the four, their faces now solemn, uneasy. 'What's the matter, boys. He's only one man an' there are four of you,' he jeered. 'Then again, Jesse Monk thought he had a winning hand.'

Teal came to his feet with an abruptness that sent the chair he had been sitting on clattering over. Anger masked his face; his right hand settled on the butt of his Colt.

'Don' push me, Quinn,' he grated darkly.

Quinn backed away, palms held out in a placatory gesture.

'Ain't no use getting riled at me, Teal,

that won't keep the Buscadero from coming after you. He's the one you gotta take care of afore it's too late, for all our sakes. Think it over, but don' take too long. Remember he's gunning for you for what you did to him earlier. Doc's death is just gonna make him all the more determined.' With a last look at the four, Quinn backed from the shack and a few minutes later the rattle of hooves announced his departure.

★　★　★

'Could you use some company, Sheriff?'

Ethan snapped up his head and squinted at the figure outlined in the doorway.

Night was fast approaching. The invisible sun sinking behind the mountains to the west flooded the main street of Greenwood with a red, Hadean glow and filled the narrow alleyways with purple shadow. Ethan sat back in his chair, one arm stretched out, hand encircling a glass on the desk top. Close by stood a half-empty bottle of whiskey.

California, not fazed by Ethan's silence, entered and sauntered across to the empty chair, dropping on to it. Blackie's tail thumped the boards a couple of times, but he remained by the stove lying with head between his front paws.

'I've allus figured that whiskey and law enforcement don' go together,' he said, tilting his hat back on his head.

'Then you figured wrong,' Ethan replied frostily. 'Sometimes it helps. Now, in answer to your question, I don't need company right now.' He stared pointedly at the youngster.

California lifted his eyebrows in a facial shrug.

'Guess you don't, Sheriff,' he agreed, and rose to his feet, tipping his hat back into position. 'Best get me some supper. See you around, Sheriff.'

Ethan grunted as he watched the youngster depart, then filled his glass from the bottle and stared hard at its golden contents. In his line of business it was a mistake to form close friendships for when something like this happened it hit hard.

In the short time he had known Doc a bond had been forged between them without him really knowing it. He had liked the little, peppery man and for him to die in such a vicious, brutal manner filled him with an inner rage.

He knew who had killed Doc, but proving it would be next to impossible. The rage coupled with frustration made him seek some kind of personal peace in the bottle.

He downed the contents of the glass in a single gulp and poured himself another.

★   ★   ★

'There's the reason, Pa. Apart from the ten thousand acres you and Uncle Seth laid claim to when you first came here, the rest of the land is undeeded.' Sam Quinn tossed a copy of the official land register on to the desk before Jackson Quinn. It had arrived on the morning stage and with the grim events of the day he had only just got around to looking at it. 'All those settlers you had run off your land had every right to be there, because in the eyes of the law it ain't your land. You just took it over without ever staking a claim.'

Jackson Quinn unrolled the document that was in the form of a map and stared at it. The map was overlaid with a grid of thousand-acre squares. Only one square was marked Circle Q. Two others, one adjoining the west boundary and the other the north boundary, were labelled, 'LT Land Holdings'.

'The land belongs to me,' he barked angrily and threw the map away. 'I fought Injuns to get it, damn near got mysel' killed on more'n one occasion.'

'That don' mean a thing, Pa. Times are different now. Without having it down on paper you can't officially claim any of it. Two sections have already been bought up by these LT people.

Two sections that the settlers laid claim to. Looks like after you had them run off they sold their claims to these Land Holding folk. Reckon if'n you don't put in an official claim real soon we're gonna find ourselves boxed in.'

'Just let 'em try,' Jackson Quinn stormed. 'I fought for this land once an' I'll do it agin.'

Sam shook his head sadly.

'The law's gonna be on the side of any settler who moves in unless you move quicker and buy up the land yourself.'

'Buy my own goddamn land?' Jackson roared, fixing his son with a steely glare.

Sam felt a wave of hopelessness wash over him.

'I keep trying to tell you, it ain't yours, Pa, unless you stake an official claim.'

'All right, I'll ride into Greenwood tomorrow.'

'Good.' Sam breathed a sigh of relief. 'In the meantime, I'll dig around, see if'n I can't find out who owns LT Land Holdings.'

His words brought a bitter laugh from the old man.

'I'd've thought that was plain by now, but I guess love is blind.'

'I ain't following you, Pa.'

'LT. Laura Treece. There's more to that little girl than meets the eye. I reckon she's determined to get her hands on the Circle Q, one way or another!'

*　*　*

He must have fallen asleep, for suddenly Ethan was jerked awake by the sound of gunfire coming from somewhere down the street. He came to his feet, grabbed the duster from a wall hook and slipped into it before taking up his shotgun and heading for the door. He staggered a little as he pulled the door open and lurched against the door-frame. His mouth felt dry and sour from the whiskey, head a tad woolly. He steadied himself and went out into the night. The cool air went someway to clearing his head.

Someone was running towards him and, as he came closer, he recognized the lanky form of Abner Grange. Abner grabbed Ethan's arm as he pulled up before him.

'It's the Bronsons, Sheriff. Mean as hell an' ready for trouble,' he panted out.

'Slow down, Abner. Who are these rannies?'

'Abe Bronson an' his three brothers, Toby, Jake an' Clem. They live up in the mountains, but every so often they come into town to get likkered up.' Abner ran a thin hand across his trembling lips. 'They're calling for you, Ethan. They don' like what you've done to the Silver Wheel. They aim to kill you for sure.'

'Then I'd best not keep them waiting,' Ethan replied grimly.

Abner grabbed Ethan's arm again.

'They're animals, Ethan. You can't

face them alone.'

'Ain't got much choice in the matter, Abner. You get yoursel' home. I'll take care of the Bronsons.'

Ethan broke away from the storekeeper's grip and headed towards the Silver Wheel. He could see a lot of movement outside the saloon, hear voices and laughter. Stepping off the sidewalk he proceeded to walk slowly down the centre of the wide road. Someone must have seen him coming for, as he approached the saloon, the batwings burst open and four men stepped out, spreading themselves across the street in his path.

They were big, untidy men clad in grubby buckskin jackets, dark, lank hair tumbling from beneath the brims of their hats. They were not young men filled with the brash arrogance of youth looking to make a reputation; these were men in their forties, seasoned and confident. Besides holstered pistols, each toted either a rifle or a shotgun that they held loosely in their arms.

'So you're the Buscadero they talk 'bout, eh?' The biggest of the four said, moving until he stood directly facing Ethan. Eyes in the thickly bearded face sparkled in the reflected light from the saloon. 'I'm called Abe Bronson.' He turned his head and spat at the ground. 'That's what I think of star-toters.' He looked back at Ethan and grinned.

By now everyone had piled from the saloon to line the sidewalk, watching in silent anticipation of what was to come.

Ethan smiled thinly.

'I don't give a damn what you think of me, but spitting in the street is agin the law here. You're under arrest!'

Maybe it was the bellow of laughter that drowned the faint swish of a lariat being whirled behind him. Maybe the whiskey had dulled his senses, blunted the edge of his usually keen awareness. Whatever the reason, he wasn't aware of it until the rope loop dropped over his shoulders and was jerked tight almost toppling him.

He managed to stay on his feet, but

the rope pinning his upper arms had also snagged the shotgun barrel trapping it against his chest.

Abe Bronson paused in his laughter and eyed Ethan.

'Would you mind repeating that, Sheriff, 'bout being under arrest afore we'uns kill you? By the way, afore you die this 'ere's my brothers Jake,' — he nodded to his right — 'Toby an' Clem.' He nodded to his left. 'An' behind you is Cousin Mo, jus' a'visitin'.' He levelled his rifle and his three brothers did the same. 'Never thought the famous Buscadero would be so easy to kill. Bye, Sheriff.'

The cocking of hammers was like a metallic explosion on the still, night air, raising a sweat on Ethan's face.

9

From the throng of gaping men fronting the Silver Wheel saloon Lucky Calhoun called out mockingly, 'Guess who's the lucky one now, Hawkesbury? Be a pure pleasure to pay the undertaker for tonight's work.'

Ethan strained forward against the rope. Only his upper arms were bound. He clawed for the Adams at his hip, dragging it free of its holster then dropped flat to the ground.

Two rifles and two shotguns bellowed and roared in unison, spitting tongues of flame and belching cordite smoke in a deadly hail of lead that was meant to cut Ethan in half. Instead, the swathe of bullets and lead shot found a second target in the rope wielding Mo.

The unfortunate man was literally torn apart in the hail of deadly lead that lifted him off his feet and threw him ten feet backwards in a gruesome explosion of flying flesh, splintered bone and spraying blood that was thankfully hidden by the night.

The gun in Ethan's hand barked once as he hit the ground catching Abe Bronson high on the right thigh a split second before the Bronsons' weapons discharged killing their cousin. Ethan was jerked along the ground as Mo was thrown backwards.

The sudden jerk sent the Adams flying from Ethan's grasp.

Limping badly, pain creasing his coarse features, Abe Bronson moved towards the helpless Ethan.

'Dammit, you made us done kill Mo,' he grated through clenched teeth. 'Never did like the sonofabitch anyway, but he wus family.' He worked the lever of the rifle as he spoke. 'This time I aim to finish what I started.' He raised the rifle to his shoulder.

'Sure would be mistake on your part if'n you try an' pull that trigger.'

The voice startled everyone even

causing Ethan to snap his head sideways.

California had appeared from the other sidewalk, stepping into the road. His Colt was still holstered at his side with his hand hovering by the butt.

'Git him!' Abe screamed hoarsely, swinging the rifle away from Ethan.

Ethan had seen fast-draw merchants many times before. He himself was considered fast, but California was in a class of his own.

Abe Bronson's cry was still echoing on the air when the youngster drew and fired with a speed and precison that made Ethan give a silent gasp.

The bullet drilled a neat hole in Abe Bronson's forehead. The back of the man's head exploded messily as the bullet made a less than neat exit. He toppled backwards, arms flying out and up and Ethan barely had time to roll out of the way as the heavy body crashed into the dirt.

The remaining Bronson brothers went for their holstered pistols, turning them on California.

The youngster threw himself down, rolling and firing, as he came on to his stomach, both hands on the Colt, arms outstretched.

Clem gave a choking gurgle and sank to his knees before toppling forward, hands gripping his throat where the bullet had entered.

Bullets ripped into the hard-packed earth as California continued to roll.

Seth went next, spinning as a slug gouged into his heart.

By now, Ethan had shaken himself free of the rope and was on his knees, hands wrapped around his shotgun.

Jake was taking a bead on the rolling California when Ethan fired. The heavy gauge shot threw the last of the Bronsons sprawling onto the sidewalk as the crowd scattered.

California ceased rolling and came to his feet, nodding his thanks at Ethan as the big lawman came upright, retrieving his Adams in the process.

All of a sudden they were the only

two left alive in the street, the onlookers magically vanished. Ethan was about to say something to California when a gun spoke from the saloon.

The angry buzz of a bullet passing close to Ethan's left ear had the big man ducking. California fired back at the doorway as both dodged across the street to seek shelter behind a wooden horse trough.

Men were crouched either side of the saloon doorway as once again the night erupted in a fusillade of shots.

Bullets tore into the far side of the trough and water jetted from half-a-dozen holes.

'You done somethin' to upset them gents, Sheriff?' California spoke for the first time as rapidly he reloaded his gun.

'Not yet, but I aim to,' Ethan snapped back. He eyed California. 'The name's Ethan an' I'm beholden to you for saving my hide.'

California smiled boyishly and winced as slugs thudded into the wall behind them.

'I guess they ain't so happy 'bout it.'

This was the moment Ethan had been waiting for, when the town hardcore rebelled against his methods. The Bronsons had provided the catalyst and now 'gun fever' had taken over.

Ethan reloaded his shotgun cursing himself for not cramming a pocket full of shotgun rounds before leaving the office. Yet another oversight to blame on the whiskey. With the shotgun loaded, he had only one cartridge left, but plenty of rounds for the Adams.

A salvo of bullets buzzed angrily around them and the big window of the two that flanked the entrance of the general store behind them shattered noisily. Luckily the force sent the shards of glass inwards and not over them.

Lights in the saloon were hurriedly doused leaving only a few night lamps on either side of the street to provide a poor, shadowy light.

Ethan belly crawled to the end of the trough in time to see shadowy figures appear from the alleyway beside the Silver Wheel.

His shotgun roared and two men screamed and went down. Figures had appeared on the veranda above the entrance of the saloon, crouching low, firing down at the trough. California returned their fire with an accuracy that sent the men fleeing for safety.

A stream of screaming saloon girls fled from an unseen exit at the far end of the saloon, disappearing into the night.

Footsteps sounded on the sidewalk to their right. California angled his gun in that direction.

'Don't shoot, Sheriff, it's me, Seth Wilkins. Figured you could use a hand.'

'Take a position, Seth. We could do with a few men,' Ethan called. 'Keep your eyes peeled on that far corner.'

'We need to flush those rannies outa there,' California observed as he reloaded.

The sound of galloping hooves coming in fast from the southern end of town drew Ethan's attention. He quickly loaded his last shotgun cartridge and waited, heart pounding.

The dark forms of at least twenty riders reined to a halt a hundred yards down the street. Ethan saw them leap from their saddles and melt into the darkness.

'Dammit, we're getting surrounded,' Ethan moaned, but his despair turned to relief when Bob Brady's voice came out of the darkness.

'I'm takin' it that you're still alive, Ethan. It's Bob Brady, an' I've brought a few boys with me. One o' my boys brought back word that the Bronsons had hit town an' were gunning for you, so we came as fast as we could.'

'Mighty welcome too,' Ethan called back.

A lull had appeared in the shooting as it became apparent that Ethan and California were no longer on their own.

'You in the saloon. Give yourselves up,' Ethan bellowed. His answer came in a rattle of gunfire.

'Be obliged if'n you an' your boys could show 'em the error o' their ways, Bob. A little fire-power perhaps,' Ethan called.

Guns roared in a deafening battery of sound and light as muzzle flashes lit up the night and bullets raked the front of the saloon shattering its windows.

Screams and cries came from the saloon as flying glass found unsuspecting victims.

As the fusillade of shots died away, Ethan said curtly to California, 'Cover me!' With that Ethan came to his feet and at a crouch ran across the road weaving from side to side.

From the doorway of the saloon, gun barrels flashed, but their owners were driven back as California emptied his gun at them.

Ethan reached the opposite sidewalk and threw himself against the wall. A bullet had grazed his shoulder in a minor flesh wound. He grabbed down a night lantern from its hook, inched towards the doorway and threw it inside following the action with a blast from his shotgun that raised howls of pain from within.

He pressed himself back against the wall, dropping the now empty shotgun and drawing his Adams.

Bob Brady and half a dozen of his men joined Ethan as a lurid, flickering orange glow spilled out through the doorway and shattered frontage. Within the saloon, the lamp thrown by Ethan had smashed against the long bar, spilling kerosene that ignited as it soaked into the dry boards of the floor.

In but a few short moments, a section of the bar was alight, tongues of crackling flame licking hungrily at the ceiling. Inside, men shouted in alarm and began choking as thick, billowing curtains of black smoke began to fill the saloon. Seconds later, men began pouring from the saloon, eyes streaming tears, guns blazing in all directions.

Ethan's Adams spoke sending two men to the ground, while from across the street, California and Seth Wilkins accounted for three more. It was enough for those remaining in the saloon. They tossed their weapons aside and ran out hands held high. The battle for and against law and order in Greenwood had been fought and law and order had won.

'I'll organize my men into a bucket chain. Gotta get that fire out afore the whole town burns down,' Bob Brady cried.

Townsfolk were beginning to appear now, and once they saw the threat of a shootout was past, they quickly joined Bob Brady and his men in fighting the fire.

Ethan found he had seven prisoners.

'Where's Calhoun?' he demanded.

'He lit out back when the fire started, him an' a few others, They had horses there ready an' waiting.'

Ethan gave a cold smile.

'Which leaves you boys drawing the short straw. Well, don' worry. I gotta nice little jail up the road apiece that'll fit you boys real well. Move it!'

California joined Ethan.

'What'll you do 'bout Calhoun, Ethan?'

Ethan shrugged. 'Calhoun's an opportunist. Moves in like the buzzards after a kill an' when the foods all gone, moves on agin. He won't be back he's long gone by now.'

'But you'll go after him?'

'Ain't much point. Calhoun lets others do the dirty work while he stays clean, If'n I arrested him the first circuit judge that he gets hauled before will let him go free for lack of evidence. Calhoun might stir up a riot, but he ain't one to take part in it. That's the reason he got the 'Lucky' handle. Here we are, boys, home sweet home,' Ethan called, as they reached the jail.

Blackie snapped at the prisoners' heels as they were marched through to the cell block and locked up for the night. After that Ethan and California joined the fire-fighting team. It took an hour before the blaze was under control leaving the Silver Wheel blackened and gutted inside.

'You did well, California, an' I'm more'n obliged,' Ethan said, pouring coffee after the two, smoke-blackened and red-eyed, had returned to the office.

'Glad I was around to be of assistance,' California said.

'So why are you here, California?'

'Just travelling through, like I said afore.'

'Fella don' get himself involved if'n he's just travelling through. You coulda' got yourself killed tonight.'

'I'm sure pleased I didn't,' California said with a tired grin.

'How long have you been outa prison?' The question froze the grin on California's face.

'Who . . . who said I bin in prison?' California stammered out.

'Fella shoots like you do an' is a real fast draw is bound to draw attention to his'sel'. Reputations travel fast an' as I've never heard of you, I reckon you've been outa circulation for a while an' to my way of thinkin' that can only mean one thing. Am I right?'

A resigned look crossed California's face and he shrugged. 'I did my time, Sheriff. I got out of Sacramento Prison a month ago an' I ain't wanted for anything else.' California climbed to his feet. 'I ain't here to make trouble, Sheriff, just a little family business to settle.'

'Hell, California, sit down, you're making the place look untidy. Let me guess, it was your gun that got you into trouble?'

'You're a sharp man, Sheriff.'

'Comes with the badge.'

'Fella called me out. I didn't want no fight, but in the end it was me or him. I winged him, but he just happened to be the son of a rich man in Sacramento. Luckily, I had witnesses to say he had done all the prodding, but money talks an' I ended up with two years in prison for defending myself.'

'It happens,' Ethan replied. 'So what

family business brings you here?' He eyed California who had reseated himself.

'My uncle was murdered here a year ago an' I aim to find the rannies who killed him,' came the grim reply.

'Who was your uncle?'

'Haynes. Sheriff Mort Haynes!'

'I'll say one thing for you, California, you're sure full of surprises,' Ethan said at length. 'Just how did you figure to pick up on a cold trail? Mort Haynes has been dead for a year. Whoever killed him is probably long gone by now.'

'Mebbe not,' California said slowly, causing Ethan to raise his eyebrows and peer questioningly at the youngster. 'My ma died while I was in prison. Pa had run out on us a year or so previous. We had a small farm, not much, but with me gone Ma couldn't manage it. The bank foreclosed on the property an' Ma had to move out. She found a room in Sacramento an' worked as a waitress in a hash house. I guess she couldn't take it. She took ill an' died.'

California looked away from Ethan's gaze.

'I'm sure sorry, California,' Ethan could see that retelling the events was distressing the boy. 'I didn't mean to open old hurts.'

California looked up, forcing a smile, a hint of wetness making his eyes sparkle.

'It's all right, Sheriff.'

'Ethan, boy, Ethan.'

'The point is that among the few things Ma left behind was a letter from Uncle Mort. In it he said he had found out something about Jackson Quinn that was going to make him a rich man. The secret lay in Lobo Canyon an' that he'd tell her all about it when he saw her next. Of course, he never did see her again; he was killed not long after sending the letter.'

'So you figured on going to Lobo Canyon an' taking up where he left off?'

'Not exactly. I don't recall ever seeing Uncle Mort. He an' pa never got on an' Ma never spoke a lot of him. I knew he was a lawman somewhere, but never knew where until I found that letter. I'm not even sure what kind o' lawman he was, but from the letter it looks as though he was going to blackmail Quinn. Whatever he found out cost him his life. I ain't looking for money, Ethan. As far as I can see Ma was let down by all the men in her life, including me. If'n I can find out who killed Uncle Mort an' why, then mebbe it'll help Ma rest easier in her grave an' make me feel better.'

Ethan eyed the youngster keenly. He had been through a lot in his young life and somehow retained an integrity and character that many would have let slip.

'I can't let you do that, California,' Ethan said quietly and California's expression became wooden and hard and he stiffened in the chair.

'I ain't too sure what you're saying, Ethan?'

'I'm saying I can't let you do that, go poking around, disturbing old ghosts, not as an ordinary citizen. Now, if'n you were an official deputy that would be a different matter altogether. How about it, California? I'm looking for a deputy, someone I can trust an' you have all the makings.'

California's expression changed to one of surprise.

'You want me as deputy?'

'Pay ain't much, the hours are lousy an' from time to time you come up agin a ranny who wants to put a bullet into you. On the plus side . . . ' He paused and frowned, 'Ain't too sure there is a plus side.'

'I'd be proud to be your deputy, Ethan.'

'Good. Then we can make the search for Mort Haynes's killer or killers official, but first we have another chore. After Doc's burial in the morning, we go looking for his killers.'

'This Link Teal *hombre*,' California said.

Ethan nodded approvingly.

'You listen an' take in what's being said. That's good. It could save your life one day.' Ethan scrabbled about in a drawer as he spoke and finally came up with a deputy's star. It was a trifle dull and tarnished from a long time of non-use. Ethan flipped it across the desk to California who caught it deftly in one hand. 'Get some rest an' I'll see you back here at first light, Deputy.'

10

Under a bright sun the body of Doc Blanchard was laid to rest in the small cemetery to the east of town. It looked to Ethan as though the whole town had turned out to pay its respects. Even Jackson Quinn, along with his son and the ever present Pete Benson, put in an appearance.

When the short ceremony was over and the mourners began to break up, Ethan ambled across to the Quinns. California followed. The star on his chest was no longer dull and dirty. It sparkled and shone with a new lease of life.

'Hold on, Quinn,' Ethan called, turning the man in his tracks.

'What can I do for you, Sheriff?' Quinn said brusquely.

'You can tell me where I can find Link Teal. I take it that he still works for you?'

'Shouldn't you be out looking for Doc's killers?'

Ethan smiled thinly. 'That's why I'm asking where Teal is to be found.'

'Leave him alone. He had nothin' to do with it.'

'I hope for your sake you're right. When the likes of Teal go down they're apt to drag others with 'em.'

Jackson Quinn stiffened, anger dancing in his eyes.

'Just what do you mean, Hawkesbury?' he demanded. 'Are you suggesting that I had something to do with Doc's death?'

'Pray that you didn't, Quinn,' Ethan returned softly, but with such restrained venom in his tone that Jackson Quinn felt a shiver of fear run icily through him, but he forced a thin smile.

'Be very careful who you accuse,' he hissed warningly.

'I always am,' Ethan replied. 'By the way, evidence has come my way that suggests I might find the reason for the late Sheriff Haynes's death in Lobo

Canyon. Something tells me that Doc's killers and Haynes's killers could be one and the same.'

A feeling that a knife was being turned in his heart gripped Quinn. For a split second his eyes widened and a sense of panic overwhelmed him, but he forced himself to remain calm.

'I won't bandy words with you, Hawkesbury. I don't recognize you as the official law in Greenwood. Set foot on my land and I'll have you shot.'

'Pa!' Sam Quinn spoke up, shocked at his father's words, but the old man was already walking away, heading towards a waiting buckboard. Ethan watched him go.

'I'm sorry, Sheriff. I don't know what's got into Pa,' Sam said.

Jackson Quinn turned as he reached the buckboard.

'Are you coming, Sam?'

'I'll be along later, Pa. Got some business to sort out first.'

Jackson Quinn glared at his son then climbed on to the buckboard. The driver set the single horse into motion and headed north out of town at a fast clip.

Sam shook his head despondently.

'I guess it's been the helluva day for all of us,' he said unhappily.

'Especially for Doc,' Ethan replied coldly and walked away, California dropped into step beside him.

'Was that wise, mentioning Lobo Canyon?'

'Ain't supposed to be wise,' Ethan retorted with a brief grin. 'Jus' supposed to stir up a hornet's nest! Come on, I'll stand you coffee at Laura's an' then we'll hit the trail.'

★   ★   ★

Sam Quinn was far from happy as Pete wheeled him into the café and after settling him at a table departed. Laura descended on the young man with an eager smile on her pretty face.

'I saw you at Doc's funeral, but knowing the way your pa feels about me

I thought it best to keep myself to myself.' Her face saddened. 'I'll miss Doc, he was a good friend.'

'Yeah. We all will,' Sam returned abruptly.

His tone confused her, but she put it down to grief.

'What can I get you, Sam?'

'The answer to a question.' His face was grim, tone suddenly unfriendly.

Her brow furrowed under his scrutiny. She had never seen him like this before.

'What is it, Sam?'

The moment he had been dreading had come. He could still turn away, but he had to know. He withdrew the folded land map from his pocket and passed it across to her.

'Take a look and you tell me,' he replied frostily.

Puzzlement still etched on her face, she unfolded the document and eyed it dutifully.

'I don't understand, Sam,' she said unhappily.

'Do you deny that LT Land Holdings stands for Laura Treece?' He demanded.

'I don't know what you mean, Sam.'

'I seem to remember you telling me that you had a hankering to buy some land around here. Seems to me that you've started,' he said accusingly.

She stared at him dumbfounded, hurt by the hostility of his look and tone. Tears sprang in her eyes. She threw the document at him.

'If'n that's what you think, Sam Quinn, then damn you!' she cried, the shrillness of her voice turning the heads of the few customers in the café. 'If I did own land around here I'd want it to be as far away from you as possible!' With that tirade delivered, she turned away and stumbled from the room.

Sam stared dumbly after her then, with a heavy heart, propelled himself to the door, upsetting a table noisily in the process, and out on to the sidewalk.

Ethan and California had witnessed

the whole scene in silence as they sat at the counter.

'I wonder what that was all about?' California murmured. He slipped from his stool and righted the table, then his eyes fell on the document that Laura had thrown back at Sam. It lay on the floor. He retrieved it and returned to the counter, opening it and spreading it out so Ethan could see.

'Looks like someone has been buying up land next to the Circle Q,' he said.

Ethan's eyes lidded as he stared thoughtfully at the map.

'Not next to it, but Circle Q land itself. I've seen it happen afore. Big ranchers like Quinn came here when the land was ripe for taking. Chased off the Indians and took it for themselves. Trouble is that some of them forgot to stake their claim, make it official. By the looks o' this the Circle Q officially owns around ten thousand acres, but when they expanded they didn't bother to make it official, just took it for granted it was theirs. Official records show the land to be unclaimed so the settlers move in.'

'An' range wars start,' California said shrewdly.

'That's about the way of it, but Quinn moved quickly. He hired the likes of Teal an' his rannies to chase off any would-be settlers before they were powerful enough to oppose him.'

'So they buy the land from the government in good faith only to find that working it could get them a real unfriendly visit from Teal. Isn't that what happened to you, Ethan?'

'That's exactly what happened to me.'

'So it looks like someone has been buying up the settlers' deeds an' is getting ready to move in on Quinn.' California nodded and his eyes sparkled as he looked at Ethan. 'LT, Laura Treece. That's why young Quinn was so all fired up. She's buying up the deeds real cheap, taking the land from under his very nose.'

Ethan gave a grim chuckle and shook his head.

'Like Sam Quinn, neither of you can see the trees for the forest.'

'How come?' California demanded.

'That little gal ain't no land-grabber, she just happens to have the same initials as the real culprit an' if'n I ain't much mistaken that person is Link Teal.'

'Teal?' California's eyes popped. 'You figure him to have the brains an' the money for such an operation?'

'Somethin's keeping him around these parts,' Ethan observed shrewdly. 'It can't be for what he's getting for doing Quinn's dirty work; I figure he's staying to protect his own interests.'

'Or someone else's,' California brooded.

'You have someone in mind?'

'Mebbe,' California said cautiously. 'Who would benefit mostly from putting Quinn outa business and at the same time getting control of Circle Q land?'

'Go on, I'm listening,' Ethan prompted.

'How 'bout the Boxed B?' California offered quietly.

Ethan almost choked on his last mouthful of coffee.

'Bob Brady?'

'Sure, why not?' California returned defensively. 'As I see it he's the only one who would gain from the Circle Q going out of business. He'd get control of the whole valley and be a pretty powerful man.'

Ethan set down his cup and climbed to his feet throwing some coins on the counter top.

'Mebbe you think too much. Let's go find ourselves some killers an' mebbe some answers.' But it was a quest that was about to be delayed by an unforeseen disaster.

Outside, Sam Quinn had wheeled himself away from the café angry with himself at the clumsy way he had handled the situation with Laura. The look of hurt on Laura's face had convinced him that she was innocent of any conspiracy. He had listened to his pa, taken his word at face value with the damning evidence of LT Land Holdings to back him up, and without even thinking it through had accused the girl he loved of a foul attempt to take over the Circle Q.

He wheeled himself rapidly along the sidewalk until one wheel caught in a gap on the worn planking and brought him to an abrupt halt. Pete Benson was not in sight.

Savagely he began rocking from side to side in an effort to free the wheel and it was at this point that Ethan and California emerged from the café.

Ethan saw the predicament the boy was in and turned to go to his aid. He was only half aware of the approaching lumber wagon drawn by a team of four. Sam was not aware of it in his anger-fed frustration to free himself.

Throwing himself against the opposite side of the chair and hauling on the trapped wheel, his weight tilted the chair to one side. The wheel lifted free of the gap and Ethan gave a gasp of concern as the chair continued to tilt. He broke into a run with California hard on his heels as the chair tilted towards the road.

They both heard Sam's cry of fear as, at the last moment, he saw the approaching wagon as the chair turned over and threw him into the wagon's path.

The wagon driver saw the young man fall and hauled back desperately on the reins trying to turn the team away from the helpless man.

The wheelchair rolled over under the hooves of the leading pair. The heavy horses reacted in panic.

The wheelchair splintered beneath their stamping hooves. One horse half turned in its traces, kicking out at the shattered wheelchair and in doing so a flying hoof caught Sam in the small of the back as he tried to drag himself to safety. He cried out in agony as he was sent crashing up against the sidewalk supports.

By now people were yelling. California dived for the horses' heads, grabbing the leather straps while Ethan pitched himself between Sam and the horses, protecting the boy, as a combination of California and the driver brought the animals under control.

The driver was down by Ethan's side in an instant.

'There was nothin' I could do, Sheriff,' he wailed unhappily.

Sam lay on his back, face grey and twisted in pain. He opened his eyes as Ethan knelt over him.

'My back,' he moaned. 'Pain!' His face contorted and his head lolled to one side.

Pete Benson broke through the gathered crowd, concern on his big, round face.

'Sam!' Laura appeared and she threw herself down beside him tears filling her eyes.

'We need to get him to a bed,' Ethan

said gently, lifting her to her feet.

'My place, Sheriff,' Laura cried, brushing away the tears.

'I'll bring him,' Pete said lifting the young man effortlessly in his arms and following Laura.

Ten minutes later with Sam safely tucked up in Laura's bed above the café, Ethan and California moved outside the room to talk.

'That boy needs a doctor real bad,' California said with a shake of his head.

Laura came from the room.

'He's got feeling back in his legs, Ethan, but he's in such pain. What are we gonna do?' She looked from one to the other, red-rimmed eyes pleading.

Ethan rubbed the back of his neck.

'Nearest sawbones is in Billings an' that's a full two-day ride away. It'd take too long.'

'So, what do you suggest?' California asked.

Hope suddenly flared in Ethan's eyes.

'I know someone who could mebbe

help an' he's a lot closer, if he'll come.'

'Another doctor?' California looked puzzled.

'Sort of. He sure helped me when I needed it. Look after the town, California. I'll be back by dawn.' Ethan said no more as he hurried away with puzzled eyes on his back.

It was a little before dawn that Ethan returned and entered the café followed by two others. Laura was there to meet him, eyes red from crying.

'He's getting worse, Ethan. Fever's got him now . . . ' Her voice tailed away as she took in Ethan's companions for the first time and her eyes widened.

'Don't let appearances fool you, girl. Meet Running Elk. Best damn Crow medicine man in the business. And his, eh, companion, White Dove.'

Running Elk smiled, saying nothing, while White Dove peered around curiously.

In the small bedroom, California and Pete Benson both showed surprise as Ethan appeared leading Running Elk and White Dove.

Sam Quinn lay in the bed. All the colour had drained from his face leaving behind a white, sweat-beaded mask.

Running Elk felt the young man's fevered brow then threw back the blankets and turned him on his side running his big, leathery hands down his back. They paused at the base of the spine. Running Elk grunted, pressed and massaged until finally there was an audible click. Sam Quinn spasmed in his fevered sleep and a cry escaped his lips. His eyes opened for a second then closed again.

Running Elk turned Sam on to his back and stood up and spoke for the first time.

'White-man's bed no good for back to mend. Only good for humping white woman. Need to lay on floor.'

A startled silence followed his words and Laura's face reddened.

'You heard the man,' Ethan spoke up quickly. 'Laura get some blankets on the floor. Pete an' California, get Sam on to them an' leave the rest to Running Elk.'

'Will he get better?' Laura spoke up.

Running Elk turned to her.

'Damn fool Indians always falling off horses and busting back. I fix many times,' he boasted proudly.

California sniffed, nose wrinkling.

'What's that smell, Ethan?' he whispered and Ethan smiled.

'Indian medicine. Reckon the stronger it smells the better it is. Sure worked for me.'

When Sam was finally laid on the floor to Running Elk's satisfaction, Ethan turned to Pete.

'Do whatever Running Elk asks if'n you wanna see Sam well agin, an' I'll be obliged you feed an' water my prisoners while I'm gone.'

'Sure thing, Ethan,' Pete responded.

'Laura, can you whip up breakfast for California and me? We got some hard riding to do an' some killers to bring to justice, one way or the other!'

Unaware of what had happened to his son, Jackson Quinn had other problems to occupy his mind. These problems increased by the time he reached the Circle Q, entered the house, to find Calhoun seated behind his desk drinking his whiskey and smoking his cigars. To make matters worse, Link Teal and his cronies were ranged about the room as though they owned the place.

'Hello, Jackson. We was wondering when you'd get back. Good burial was it?' Calhoun jetted smoke and smiled amiably.

Quinn's temper exploded.

'What the damn hell do you think you're doing, Calhoun?' he raged. 'Get outa my house. All of you get out!' he thundered, voice thick with anger. 'I thought I'd seen the last of you. I heard the saloon burned down.' He glared at Calhoun.

'Kinda touchy, ain't he?' Dawson

spoke up, grinning his infuriating, toothy smile.

'Things woulda gone different if'n that California hadn't poked his nose in,' Calhoun growled angrily; then his face lightened and he smiled. 'Ain't no sense worryin' 'bout it now though.' He flicked cigar ash on to the floor.

'You've gone too far this time, Calhoun. I'll see your worthless hide nailed to the wall for this, that goes for all of you. Hawkesbury's looking for you all an' by God I won't stand in his way this time.'

Teal smiled. 'That's what we're countin' on, ol' man. You sending him to where we'll be waiting.'

'I wouldn't lift a finger to help any of you.'

'Wrong, Jackson. You'll do exactly as we say. You see, we know all about Lobo Canyon and what you did.' Calhoun grinned at the stricken look that filled Quinn's face. 'Mort Haynes knew and was blackmailing you that's why you hired Link here to get rid of him. Mort wasn't too keen on dying, so he told Link everything, but it didn't save him. Link weren't too sure what to do wi' the information so he brought it to me.'

Quinn's face grew ashen. He sucked in a deep breath.

'What do you want, Calhoun?' he asked thickly.

'The Circle Q,' Calhoun replied softly.

'That you'll never get.'

'Oh, I think I will unless you want to end your days in prison. Reckon a trade of information with the Buscadero will put me in a better light. All you've got to do is sign over the deeds of the Circle Q to me. You an' your son can stay here an' run the place, only this time I'll be the silent partner. O' course we'll need a proper, legal document turning the place over to me should anything happen to you. This way only you an' me need know 'bout it. You keep your freedom an' Lobo Canyon gets forgotten.' Again, Calhoun tapped cigar ash on to the floor.

'You've got it all worked out, haven't
you?' Quinn sneered, but the fight had
gone out of his voice.

'Mostly,' Calhoun agreed smugly.
'Mind you, I had a few bad moments
when I found out that you didn't own
all the land that the Circle Q covers.
Mighty careless of you, Jackson, but
Link an' his boys soon showed them
settlers the error of their ways and I was
able to buy their deeds for next to
nothing.'

Quinn's head snapped up.

'So you an' the Treece woman are in
it together!'

It was Calhoun's turn to look
puzzled.

'What are you talking about?'

'LT Land Holdings. Laura Treece.'

'Damn me, I never thought of that,'
Calhoun said.

'You mean you an' she ain't partners?'

Calhoun laughed and shook his head.

'When you get things wrong, Jackson,

you do it in a big way. The only partnering I do with a woman is when she's on her back,' Calhoun said coarsely, bringing more laughter from Teal and his men. 'LT is me, ol' man. Lucky Tom, Lucky Tom Calhoun!'

Quinn sagged visibly. 'You won't get away with it, Calhoun,' he said faintly.

'You let me worry 'bout that. Just you remember that if'n I don't get away with it you'll spend the rest of your days rotting in prison. Look on the bright side: you'll still run the Circle Q, not even your son will have to know. The only fly in the ointment is Hawkesbury. He's a man dedicated to the truth. Once he's outa the way all our problems will be over. So what do you say, Jackson, are we partners?'

'You leave me little choice,' Quinn said brokenly.

'No, I don't an' that's how I like it. I want you to lead the Buscadero to Lobo Canyon and we'll take care of him there.' Calhoun came to his feet. 'Don't let me down, Jackson, or it'll be all the worse for you. If'n *I* lose, *you* lose. Come on, boys, let's leave the man in peace.'

For a long time afterwards, Jackson Quinn stood at the big window, staring out across the vast rolling, green range of Circle Q land that ended at the distant mountains. A broken man, he waited for Ethan Hawkesbury to come, ready to tell all. When he didn't show it seemed to Quinn that everything was against him.

When darkness fell, unaware of the reason for the lawman's non-appearance, Quinn lit the table lamp, fetched a bottle of whiskey and sat down at the desk placing pen and paper before him. He drank and wrote and it was late by the time he sealed the letter in an envelope and addressed it simply 'Hawkesbury' and sat back in the chair. But even then he was not finished.

On a second sheet of paper he

scrawled the words, *Forgive me, son* and let the pen fall from his trembling fingers. There were tears in his eyes. He would die before he let the likes of Calhoun steal the Circle Q.

11

The sun had cleared the eastern rimrock when Ethan and California with Blackie loping ahead, rode out of Greenwood heading north A hearty breakfast had made the early morning chill more tolerable.

Ethan hunkered down in his duster, collar turned up, hat pulled down, saying nothing and California, draped in a colourful poncho did nothing to break his big companion's concentration. When Ethan did finally speak it had nothing to do with the problems that lay ahead of them.

'Who taught you to use a gun, California?'

Ethan's voice snapped the youngster out of his own thoughts and he glanced sideways over the upturned collar of his coat at the lawman.

'Can't rightly say it was anyone but

me'sel, Ethan. I jus' seem to have a natural talent with a gun.' He gave a wry smile. 'Guess it turned out to be more of a curse. I never had a hankering to prove me'sel, but after winning a couple county fair fast-draw competitions, word sorta got around and suddenly I found me'sel getting called out by rannies wanting to prove themselves.'

Ethan nodded. 'There's always someone wanting to be top dog.'

'Too many someones,' California agreed. 'It gets awful hard to keep walking away from challenges.' A bitter note crept into California's voice. 'The one time I didn't it cost me two years of freedom an' my ma's life.'

They lapsed into silence as the rising sun burnt away the last pockets of mist and filled the air with the warm scents of the earth. By the time they reached the Circle Q, both men had folded back their collars against the rising heat.

Expecting to be braced by Quinn's men, Ethan was surprised to find the yard before the sprawling, timber-built ranch house empty. The bunkhouse, too, was empty showing signs of a hurried departure by its former occupants in the form of unmade bunks and litter on the floor.

'Sure is quiet,' California commented, as he swung down from his calico, eyes ranging about suspiciously.

'Too quiet,' Ethan growled.

The door into the house was partly open. Ethan mounted the veranda, hefting his Adams as he approached it. He motioned California to take up a position on one side of the door before using a booted foot to open it completely, leaping to one side as he did so.

Silence!

No hail of bullets greeted his arrival. Throwing California a puzzled glance, Ethan entered followed by California. A few minutes later they found the sole, tragic occupant.

Jackson Quinn sat at his desk. Sometime during the night he had placed the barrel of a .45 in his mouth and blown off the back of his head. It answered the question of the empty bunkhouse. Many of the Circle Q hands had more than questionable pasts. They had no doubt heard the single gunshot, found Quinn dead and decided not to stay.

Ethan found the blood-spattered envelope addressed to him and tore it open. He read it silently before passing it over to California. In it Quinn told of the death of Mort Haynes and Doc Blanchard at the hands of Link Teal. It also told of Calhoun's involvement, LT Land Holdings and finally of Calhoun's plan to lure Hawkesbury into Lobo Canyon where Teal and his men would be waiting in ambush. It told everything in a damning document that would hang Teal, his men and Calhoun; or, almost everything; it never told why Mort Haynes was killed or what the secret of Lobo Canyon was.

'Lucky Tom Land Holdings,' California said at length as he passed the letter back to Ethan. 'We were all wrong.' He shook his head before nodding towards the second note. 'I guess that one's for Sam. So what do we do now, Ethan?'

There was a grim, hard mask to Ethan's face now that told the young man that he would not like the answer.

'Let's not disappoint Calhoun and Teal. Somehow this all began in Lobo Canyon, now it's gonna end there.'

California was right, he did not like the answer, but followed the Buscadero from the house with its smell of death out into the fresh, clean air.

Ethan turned and faced California as they reached their horses.

'I can't ask you to come with me, California. I could get my fool head blown off an' I wouldn't like the same to happen to you.'

'Mort Haynes was family, Ethan; I'm coming,' California stated as he swung into the saddle. ' 'Sides, I'm a deputy now.'

A smile twitched Ethan's lips as he climbed into the saddle.

'Then let's go, deputy.'

★   ★   ★

Lobo Canyon was a deep, sheer-sided split in the rugged hills to the north-west of the Circle Q. Here the land was broken and furrowed with brush-choked ravines and gullies topped here and there with stands of stunted trees that wrapped twisted roots around exposed rock.

From where they hunkered down behind the cover of a stand of oak, Ethan and California could look right into the mouth of the canyon. But the canyon dog-legged to the left giving them only a limited view of what lay inside.

'As I recall from the map in the office, Lobo Canyon is a box canyon,' Ethan said softly. 'One way in an' the same way out.'

'The perfect place for an ambush,'

California observed drily. 'So what do we do, Ethan?'

'Sit an' watch an' go in just afore nightfall keeping in the shadows, see if'n we can't get a little surprise on our side.'

'D'yer think Calhoun and Teal are waiting for us somewhere inside?'

'An' then some. We picked up a whole passel of tracks back a ways heading in this direction. How many do you reckon?'

'Eight, ten riders.'

' 'Bout what I figured,' Ethan said, bobbing his head in agreement.

'Two agin ten. If'n I was a betting man I know who I'd put my money on,' California said morosely.

Ethan gave a chuckle.

'It ain't always the biggest army that wins the battle.'

'Is that Buscadero philosophy, Ethan?' California asked, raising an eyebrow.

'Somethin' like that,' Ethan agreed. 'Say, where's that hound got to?'

They both looked around for Blackie. The dog had loped ahead as they had ridden to the canyon and now was nowhere to be seen.

'Let's hope it keeps its head down,' California said.

Ethan motioned with his head and the two withdrew through the narrow belt of straggly oak into the shallow draw behind where their horses cropped on a patch of grass. Ethan found a couple of strips of dry, leathery jerky in his saddle-bags and handed one to California.

The two chewed in silence, both lost in their own thoughts. California had climbed high enough on the side of the draw to peer through the tree-line at the high canyon rim.

'There's at least one ranny on the rim. Seen him move a couple times,' he called back to Ethan.

Ethan was looking towards California when an amused voice, accompanied by the metallic click of a hammer being thumbed back, called, 'Mighty nice of you boys dropping in like this. Easy, lawdogs, or you'll die where you stand!' The last sentence was a raised-voice warning as Ethan whirled to face the owner of the voice, hand freezing halfway towards his holstered gun. California slithered down the side of the draw, joining Ethan, hands raised to chest level, palms outwards. 'Lucky said to keep an eye out for you as you might get lost an' need a little help finding him.' Chuck Dawson smiled his toothy grin and looked down at them from the other side of the draw. He was flanked on either side by two other men, one toting a shotgun. The latter Ethan recognized as a two-bit outlaw by the name of Griff Reynolds.

'Real neighbourly o' him,' Ethan muttered.

'That's ol' Lucky, all heart. Now shuck the irons, lawdogs, an' do it real easy as I got a terrible twitchy finger.' He grinned happily at the thought, eyes fixed firmly on the two.

'Better do as the man says, California,' Ethan said.

'Use two fingers. Man fisting a butt is likely to be tempted into having a go an' such foolishness we can do wi'out.' Both hesitated and Dawson's grin broadened. 'Mebbe you're feeling lucky?' He raised an eyebrow.

Ethan said nothing. Slowly, using thumb and forefinger he eased his Adams from its holster and, holding it out at arm's length, he let it drop to the ground and California followed suit.

'Damn, got the famous Buscadero in my sights. Jus' a little squeeze on the trigger and . . . ' Dawson taunted.

The deep, thoaty snarl, when it came, took all of their attention.

Reynolds, to the right of Dawson, snapped his head around in time to see a black shadow with gaping, tooth-filled jaws leap out of the ground towards him. He half turned, giving out a bellow of fear, raising one hand from his shotgun to throw a protective arm across his face.

The jaws snapped down on the arm and held as the rest of Blackie's body slammed into Reynolds sending him sideways to cannon into Dawson.

Dawson's gun exploded sending a bullet into the dirt at Ethan's feet.

California reacted instantly. He dived on his Colt and rolled rapidly to his left as the gun to Dawson's left tried to bring his weapon into play as Dawson collided into him.

The Winchester cracked, gouging the earth where California had been only seconds before.

California rolled over three times before coming to a halt, belly down. Gripping the Colt in two hands, he fired off two shots. The gunman jerked as both bullets ripped into his body and punched fist-sized exit holes in his back that sprayed blood and flesh over the rocks before he toppled down the side of the draw and lay still.

Dawson was down on his knees, ignoring Reynolds who was screaming and yelling, thrashing about on his back with Blackie on top of him.

Cursing, Dawson attempted to line up his gun on Ethan, but by this time Ethan had scooped up his weapon and had opened fire.

Three slugs caught Dawson in the forehead in a deadly display of rapid fire accuracy. Dawson's hat flew into the air with most of the gunman's head still in it while the rest of his body fell forward and hung over the edge of the draw pumping a torrent of blood down the steep side.

Ethan charged up the side of the draw and called Blackie off the unfortunate Reynolds who lay there moaning and gripping an arm that pumped blood from a series of deep lacerations.

'Help me,' he whimpered, as Ethan's shadow fell across him.

The man was in a bad way, but there was no compassion in Ethan's eyes as he looked down at him.

'You've caused a lotta grief in your time, Reynolds, let your friends help you,' he said, and turned away.

'Bastard!' the man shrilled.

Ethan heard the hammer of a pistol being thumbed. He turned. Reynolds had risen to his knees holding his injured arm against his bloodsoaked front and drawn his gun.

Ethan fired once, the bullet smashing ribs on its way to Reynolds's heart. A look of surprise filled the outlaw's eyes. He rocked back on his calves, the gun slipping from his bloodstained hand as he toppled sideways and lay still.

'Ethan, we got company!' California called urgently.

Riders were coming in from the west, four of them, appearing and disappearing as the land rose and fell.

Ethan slithered down the side of the draw and ran towards his mount, California was already in the saddle.

'There are times when a retreat is called for an' this is one of them,' he said, as he forked his horse and, seconds later, the two of them galloped eastwards following the line of the draw.

As they charged out of the draw, Ethan didn't need California's pointing finger to show him four horsemen galloping in from the east, guns blazing, but the distance was too great yet to cause them any concern.

Ethan reined his horse on a course that headed straight for the canyon.

'I don' think this is a good idea, Ethan,' California shouted above the galloping hooves of their own mounts.

'Neither do I,' Ethan replied grimly.

They entered the canyon and Ethan motioned California to ride down the right-hand side while he took the left. Blackie had joined them and raced away excitedly down the centre.

They rounded the bend and found themselves in a wide, circular area surrounded on all sides by sheer, hundred-foot walls with no exit but by the way they had entered.

Ethan peered upwards. Men had appeared on the canyon rim, rifles in their hands and the growing echo of hoofbeats announced the imminent arrival of their pursuers.

They were trapped!

A rifle cracked from the rim above and dirt puffed a few yards ahead of Ethan's snorting horse, causing the animal to back nervously.

Blackie's excited barking turned California's head as he reined his calico towards Ethan. Blackie stood before the dark entrance to a cave. A bullet whined off a rock close to the hound and he turned and bounded into the cave.

'There's a cave in the rear wall, Ethan,' California called, dragging his Winchester from its saddle boot and kneeing the calico forward. Ethan wheeled his horse and followed the younger man as more rifles spat lead from above.

They reached the cave and dived inside leaving the horses to fend for themselves. A hail of lead followed them inside.

'Do you get the impression they wanted us in here?' California said, crouched against one wall of the cave, casting a glance to where Ethan was positioned the other side.

'Sure seems that way.' Ethan peered around. The cave went back about twenty feet and, where the shadows gathered, he thought he could make out the opening of a tunnel.

'You ain't as smart as I thought, Ethan,' Calhoun's voice floated in from outside. 'That retirement o' yours musta taken the edge offa your thinking. You an' that pup wi' you are jus' where I wanted you. Something you should know 'bout them caves, Ethan, they're like Lobo Canyon: only one way in an' one way out an' they's both the same, which from where I'm standing don' look too good for you. I'm glad the old man gave you the message of where to find us.'

'He did more than that, Calhoun. He wrote it all down an' signed it,' Ethan shouted back.

'Ain't too smart a thing to do if'n he wants to stay outa prison.'

215

'He was a lot smarter than you gave him credit for. The Circle Q will never be yours, Calhoun, he made dead sure of that.' Ethan smiled grimly at his own joke, one that was lost on Calhoun.

'He knows the consequences. Prison if'n he's lucky, though more'n likely he'll hang.'

'He made sure of that as well. He shot himsel' last night, Calhoun, so whatever hold you might have had on him is gone. Your luck's deserted you, Tom Calhoun. This time you've lost an' that goes for the men with you.'

There was a moment's silence following Ethan's words.

'Mebbe, but you won't be around to find out one way o' the other. You're about to retire, this time permanently. An' if'n I can't have the Circle Q, then nobody will,' Calhoun returned harshly.

Guns began blazing away outside, firing into the cave mouth causing the two to retreat deeper into the cave and seek shelter behind some low rock slabs as bullets ricocheted around them.

The air became filled with the angry whine and screech of deflected bullets. When finally the shooting stopped, the sound continued in the pair's minds.

Outside, two men waited either side of the cave entrance, each carried a bundle of red dynamite sticks bound tightly together. As the shooting ceased, the two lit their fuses, moved to either side of the cave entrance and threw them inside then retreated rapidly.

As the two bundles, with their spluttering, smoking fuses, hit the cave floor, Ethan was up on his feet and, hauling the still-dazed California upright, pushed the young man into the tunnel and followed quickly. After a few yards, he hollered at California to get down, at the same time throwing himself down and covering his ears. A few seconds later a terrific double explosion ripped the air apart. Walls and floor shook, the blast riding over Ethan's sprawled body in a series of buffeting waves.

It was followed almost immediately

by a rumbling, grating roar and Ethan felt rather than saw the cloud of dust that rolled down the tunnel from the cave as the cave roof collapsed shutting off what little light there was, sealing them in forever. He hunched a shoulder and pulled the collar edge of his duster around to hold over his nose and mouth. Ahead, he could hear California coughing and spluttering in the choking darkness.

'Cover your mouth and nose. Dust'll settle soon,' Ethan called out, voice muffled.

It was a good ten minutes before Ethan uncovered his nose and could breathe normally.

'Got any good ideas on how to get out of this place?' California called.

'I'm working on it,' Ethan replied, feeling in his pocket where he kept a few lucifers. Extracting one he struck it on the wall and in the flaring light he saw the white blob of California's face a few yards ahead. Gathering up his shotgun and holding the match aloft he moved to California's side and sank down beside him as the flame on the splinter of wood reached his fingers and he dropped it. The light winked out and the heavy darkness settled once again over the pair.

'I hope you've got a lot of those,' California said.

'Not enough, so we'll have to improvise. You seen anythin' of Blackie?' As if in answer to his question, a distant barking came from a long way ahead.

'Damn hound seems to have more lives than a cat,' California commented.

'Gonna have to make a torch o' some kind if'n we're to see where we're going,' Ethan said and began ripping at the hem of his duster, tearing off inch-wide strips. These he knotted together and wrapped around the end of his shotgun barrel in a thick, tight ball. Scraping a second lucifer into life he applied it to the linen ball. Tiny flames danced up from the material to provide them with a dim light.

California looked impressed.

'Now I know why you wear a duster,' he joked, following Ethan up as the big lawman clambered to his feet.

'Won't last long, but it might stop us stepping into somethin' that ain't there, like a hole.'

With Ethan in the lead they started down the tunnel that was no wider than the width of two men and not as high, causing the taller Ethan to bend.

After five minutes, Blackie came bounding out of the darkness ahead. He ran between their legs, tail wagging and barking before darting ahead. They found him a few minutes later sitting patiently by a tumble of rocks that sloped away from the side wall.

'Looks like another tunnel that's fallen in,' California observed.

Blackie barked, came to his feet and pawed at the rock fall.

'I think he's trying to tell us something,' Ethan mused.

'I don't reckon this to be a natural rock fall. Seems man-made to me,'

California said. He began pulling at the upper rocks until he had cleared a hole big enough to wriggle through. Blackie scrambled up and followed him through. 'I can see light ahead!' California called back excitedly.

12

Ethan one-handedly enlarged the opening and dragged himself through, clawing his way down the slope the other side until he reached level ground. He shook the burning linen ball from the end of his shotgun as the wrappings parted and flared briefly.

A dim light showed ahead blocked only by California as he made his way towards it. Crouching low in a much lower and less wide tunnel, Ethan followed, and a minute later joined the youngster in a tall, cathedral-like cavern that Ethan estimated to be a least sixty feet high and half that across.

Such light as there was came from way up in the high roof; a narrow crack no more than three or four inches wide and a foot long that probably opened on the canyon rim. Below it gleamed a dark pool of water.

'Least we won't die of thirst,' California said glumly as he made his way towards it, weaving between a litter of boulders and rock slabs that were strewn about the cavern floor. In the dull, gloomy light, Ethan could see that there were no other openings. 'Jesus!' California's alarmed voice echoed about the cavern. He was staring at something on the floor hidden from Ethan's sight.

The big lawman hurried across and sucked in his breath in surprise.

They had been dead a long time. Two skeletons clad in fragments of clothing. Only by the clothing could Ethan make out that one was male and the other female.

'Dammit, now I know there's no way out,' California muttered darkly.

'I don't think these folk were in a position to look,' Ethan said grimly, as he hunkered down next to the male skeleton. There was a hole in its forehead and the back of the skull was missing. Next to him there was enough material clinging to the ribs of the female skeleton to determine a hole in the region of the heart. 'They were dead before they arrived.' He straightened, knees creaking loudly.

'Who were they and how'd they get here?' California asked.

Ethan bent down and lifted something that was half buried in the sandy soil at his feet. It was a leather wallet, but it was empty. The only clue to its owner were the initials on the front that had been burnt into the leather: S.Q.

'S.Q.,' he said out loud.

'It means something to you?'

'If'n I'm right, the answer to a lot of questions. Seth Quinn, Jackson Quinn's brother. Seth Quinn ran off with his brother's wife, so the story goes, only I reckon he didn't. Looks to me like Jackson Quinn caught them before they left.'

'He killed them an' brought the bodies here?' California's eyes were popping.

'An' invented the story to explain

their disappearance. I guess that's what Mort Haynes found out and was using his discovery to blackmail Quinn with.'

'So Quinn had Uncle Mort killed.'

'But afore he died, Teal an' his cronies tortured the truth outa him an' took the knowledge to Calhoun. Calhoun was far more greedy than Mort Haynes. He wanted the Circle Q. He bought up land all around it and came in to claim the main prize itself. Quinn knew he would lose everything if'n he remained alive an' the shame would be left to Sam, so he took the only course left open. Taking his own life has put an end to Calhoun's dream. He'll never get his hands on the Circle Q now.' Ethan's forehead furrowed. 'I don' like it, California. Calhoun's lost an' he don't take losing lightly.'

'D'yer think he'll go after Sam?'

'It'll be the only way he can get the Circle Q. Kill Sam an' take over. I know Calhoun. He can fake up papers to fool any lawyer an' with Sam outa the way, ain't no one gonna be around to argue the point. There's gotta be a way outa here somewhere an' we've gotta find it quick.'

It took an hour of searching to finally convince the pair that Calhoun had spoken the truth about there being no way out of the cave system.

Ethan stood in the cavern and peered up at the high roof.

'D'you think you can climb up to the crack?' he said after a lengthy silence.

California shrugged his lips after a brief study of the rough wall and glanced at Ethan.

'Reckon so. What have you got in mind?'

'As I see it, the roof is the weak link. There are cracks up there, hairline ones, but you can jus' make 'em out.' He removed his duster as he spoke and tore off an eight by twelve-inch strip that he proceeded to lay on a rock slab. 'All it needs is a little persuasion an' we might get a hole we can climb out.'

'How you gonna persuade it?' California asked.

Ethan laid a handful of shotgun cartridges on the slab and began to open them, pouring the gunpowder on to the cloth.

'I'm gonna make us a stick o' dynamite an' you're gonna put it in that crack an' blow us an exit door.'

It took Ethan twenty minutes to roll the explosive contents of ten cartridges into a crude four by one-inch tube that he tied off at each end. Tearing narrow strips from the duster, he rubbed gunpowder into them and knotted them together to form a long, linen fuse that would reach from floor to roof.

California watched the whole proceedings with growing admiration. When it was his turn, he scaled the wall with comparative ease for there were hand and footholds aplenty on the rough surface.

'Wedge it in tight now,' Ethan called from below and California complied as best he could. By the time he returned to Ethan's side, the youngster's face was sheened with sweat.

'Is this gonna work, Ethan?' he asked huskily.

Ethan pulled out a lucifer.

'Only one way to find out. Take Blackie an' get in the tunnel.' Ethan waited for the two to reach the tunnel and lit the fuse.

Flame, aided by the gunpowder raced up the fuse at an alarming rate. Ethan barely had time to reach the tunnel when a tremendous explosion rent the air. Magnified by the confines of the tunnel, the sound reverberated around them, shaking the tunnel walls.

From the cavern, came a grating rumble that sounded like the whole mountain was collapsing. On their knees already, they threw themselves flat as a billowing cloud of dust and flying rock fragments filled the tunnel.

When at last an uneasy silence settled, Ethan cautiously raised himself in drifting clouds of dust that fell from his clothing, and edged back into the cavern. The entire roof of the cavern now covered the floor and he looked up into blue sky.

California let out a whoop and thumped Ethan on the back.

'You did it, Ethan, you did it.'

'Get up there, boy, an' take a look-see.'

California needed no second bidding. He scrambled up the side of the cavern and hauled himself on to the canyon rim. Soon his voice was floating down to Ethan.

'I can see down into the canyon, Ethan, an' our mounts are still there.'

'Get my saddle rope an' get us outa here.'

It took California almost another hour to find a way down into the canyon and back again. By the time he returned, Ethan had used the remainder of his duster to fashion a sling for Blackie. The hound looked remarkably miserable as California hauled him up, but his canine self reasserted itself as soon as its paws touched solid rock.

A few minutes later, Ethan joined

them at the top.

'I ain't never seen a duster used for so many different things. Gotta get me one,' California enthused with a laugh.

Ethan looked down into the hole that had once been a cavern.

'Guess they're truly buried now. Let's get outta here an' go tell Calhoun his luck's finally deserted him.'

★ ★ ★

They saw the smoke long before they reached the Circle Q. The house was on fire and too far gone to do anything but let the flames burn themselves out.

There were a number of bodies strewn about the yard, some of whom Ethan recognized as being with Calhoun earlier, but there were six others clad in leather chaps who were strangers to him. As his eyes roved over the grim death scene, it was not difficult to piece together a picture of what had happened.

'Guess some of Quinn's more loyal

hands came back from gathering the herd together for the drive to market, just as Calhoun was firing the ranch. Probably been out all night an' got fed up waiting for someone to come an' spell 'em,' Ethan said.

'Why burn the house?' California asked.

'Get rid of the fact that Quinn killed himself an' any incriminating documents that might have been left.' The sun was sinking low to the west as Ethan wheeled his horse about. 'Let's hope we ain't too late.'

At a gallop the two headed towards Greenwood.

★ ★ ★

'Hawkesbury's dead. Him an' his sidekick gunned down Jackson Quinn an' a dozen Circle Q riders afore we caught him burning the ranch down to hide the evidence. We cornered him an' he died wi' his deputy in the blaze.' Calhoun's voice rang out to the crowd of townsfolk gathered before the sheriff's office.

'I don' believe it!' Abner Grange reflected the general feeling of the townsfolk.

Calhoun eyed the man. He was the one to convince. Get him on his side and the rest would follow.

'He took us all in.' Calhoun sounded almost apologetic.

'What were you doing at the ranch?' Abner asked suspiciously.

Calhoun pulled a document from his pocket and held it up.

'Jackson Quinn and I were in business together, that's why Hawkesbury tried to shut me down. He was buying up land around the Circle Q. I reckon Doc Blanchard found out an' that's why Hawkesbury killed him.'

The statement rocked Abner back on his heels.

'I still can't believe it,' he said weakly.

'And I won't ever believe it!' Laura Treece pushed herself to the front of the group, face hostile.

Calhoun shrugged.

'He was a good man in his time, but he was getting old, losing his edge. Think back: he turned up here, took over as sheriff an' played on his reputation to scare folk into going along wi' him. How's young Sam? I heard he had an accident?'

'He's doing fine. He's sleeping.'

'That's good. The poor boy's gonna need all the help we can give him when he hears the news.'

There were nods all around and Calhoun smiled to himself. All was going to the plan he had conceived after riding away from Lobo Canyon. In fact, as things were working out, it was better than his original scheme, for now he would take over the town and the Circle Q. He did not expect much resistance from the crippled Sam Quinn and, when the time was right, Sam Quinn would meet with another unfortunate 'accident'.

'Ethan was a good man, he wouldn't do any of those things,' Laura flared.

'Hush, girl. Tend your patient and leave the running of the town to us,' Abner said.

'You're fools, all of you,' Laura said heatedly, and turned away, pushing back through the crowd.

'She's just upset,' Calhoun said tolerantly. 'In any case, Floyd Tupper is returning as your sheriff. Floyd, show yourself.'

There were a few groans from the crowd as Tupper swaggered from the sidewalk where Link Teal, along with Cal Roach and Brad Stiles and four other riders, joined by the seven prisoners from the jail, lounged in grim silence.

'You folks can rest easy. The proper law is back now,' Tupper declared grandly.

'Thank you, Floyd.' Calhoun grimaced. 'In the meantime, I intend to make a full investigation into all that's happened an' I'll be pleased if you, Abner, as one of our leading citizens, would assist me.'

Abner Grange preened under the praise. Calhoun had won.

'I'd be pleased to,' Abner said.

Calhoun nodded. Now was the time to back off and let the good folks of Greenwood chew over what he had said. Under Abner Grange's direction, he already knew the outcome.

'Well, I'll let you folks get about your business. I'll talk to you agin tomorrow, Abner.'

'Sure thing, Mr Calhoun,' Abner agreed.

Calhoun smiled as the crowd began to break up. Life had turned sweet again. Everything was going his way.

As the rays of the setting sun sent shafts of red angling through the alleyways on the western side of town and filled the store fronts with drifts of purple shadow, Calhoun turned away with Tupper at his side.

'Dammit, Calhoun, you almost had me believing.'

The amused voice froze Calhoun to the spot and stopped the crowd as they moved away in groups.

Calhoun turned slowly as Ethan Hawkesbury, shotgun stock resting on his left hip, right hand hovering by the butt of his holstered Adams, stepped from the shadows on to the dusty, rutted earth of the street.

'I swear that boy could sweet-talk a rattler into biting its own tail.'

California emerged from an alleyway ten yards to Ethan's left, thumbs stuck nonchalantly behind the buckle of his gunbelt.

There was a moment of stunned disbelief.

'How . . . how . . . ? For once in his life Calhoun could not find the words.

'He speaks Injun,' California joked.

'Kill them!' Calhoun shrieked clawing for his own weapon.

Tupper, in the meantime, had raised his hands above his head, face grey with fear.

'Don' shoot!' he screeched and all hell broke loose.

Ethan fired the shotgun one-handed,

clearing leather with the Adams at the same time.

Calhoun took the full blast. The heavy shot caught him mid chest sending up shredded clothing, flesh and blood in a gory fan. For one awful second, the rib-cage appeared as skin and muscle was ripped away. Then Calhoun was lifted off his feet in a spraying curtain of blood and slammed down on his back, dead before he hit the ground.

Tupper was hit from behind as the outlaws on the sidewalk opened up on the two, the townsfolk scattering for cover.

The Adams chattered in Ethan's big fist and three outlaws went down screaming, among them Brad Stiles.

California accounted for four more including Cal Roach, the last of Teal's men in the savage but short-lived battle.

Bullets flew like angry wasps in both directions shattering windows on either side of the street.

Demoralized by the appearance of Ethan and California and the death of Calhoun, the outlaws were no match for the two. In a battle that lasted no more than thirty seconds and left nine men dead, the remaining seven that included Teal, threw their guns down and raised their hands. Behind the drifting clouds of acrid gunsmoke, Teal stepped off the sidewalk, hands held high.

'I ain't shooting. It was Calhoun's idea.'

'Pick up your gun, Teal,' Ethan ordered grimly.

'I demand the right to a trial,' Teal shouted.

'You're getting one. Give him his gun, California, an' make sure it's loaded.'

Silently California did as he was asked and slipped the gun into Teal's holster.

'I ain't gonna draw: it'll be murder,' Teal shouted, sweat on his face.

'I'm giving you more of a chance

than you gave Doc,' Ethan replied remorselessly.

Teal looked around at the set faces of the townsfolk.

'It was Dawson an' the others.' Cautiously Teal lowered his hands, licking dry lips. There was no mercy in their eyes. 'Damn you!' he shrieked at Ethan and went for his gun.

The Buscadero waited until Teal had cleared leather before making his own draw. Teal died with two bullets in his heart, gun unfired.

Ethan turned away as Abner Grange hurried over.

'Ethan, I . . . '

'Later, Abner, I'll talk to you later. See to this mess,' Ethan said coldly and moved past the man, heading towards the remaining outlaws, a grim look on his face as he herded them into the jail.

'What do we tell Sam about his pa an' what happened to his ma?' California questioned, as later the two headed for the café.

Ethan looked at the young face.

'Nothin'. The boy'll have enough grief wi' his pa dead. Leave the ghosts of the past alone. Jackson Quinn died defending his home from Calhoun, which ain't no lie. The boy can be proud of his pa.'

California grinned.

'That sits right wi' me.'

Sam Quinn was awake when Ethan and California entered the bedroom, but only just, roused by the shooting.

'What's going on, Ethan?' he asked weakly.

'Just a little positive law enforcement, nothin' to worry 'bout. You get some rest.'

Sam nodded and turned his head to Laura who was seated at his side.

'Ain't she something?' he breathed.

'That's for sure,' Ethan agreed and Laura blushed, but her eyes were sparkling as Sam slipped back into sleep.

'He's got the feeling back in his legs, Ethan. Running Elk reckons he'll be able to walk in a few weeks. Seems that first fall he had knocked some bones outa place in his back an' that second kick put them back.'

Ethan wrinkled his nose.

'Smell o' that Injun medicine is enough to make him start running as soon as he wakes.' He looked across at Running Elk as the others laughed. 'Thanks, my friend.'

'We forgot Blackie,' California piped up. 'We tied him up at the end of town.'

As the two walked through the darkened town towards the sound of a distant, mournful baying, California asked, 'Will you stay on here as sheriff, Ethan?'

'Reckon a man needs to settle down in one place eventually, but I'll be needing a deputy.'

California grinned in the darkness.

'I can't wait to find out what you'll do wi' a duster next.'

A TOWN CALLED TROUBLESOME

John Dyson

Matt Matthews had carved his ranch out of the wild Wyoming frontier. But he had his troubles. The big blow of '86 was catastrophic, with dead beeves littering the plains, and the oncoming winter presaged worse. On top of this, a gang of desperadoes had moved into the Snake River valley, killing, raping and rustling. All Matt can do is to take on the killers single-handed. But will he escape the hail of lead?

RODEO RENEGADE

Ty Kirwan

When English couple Rufus and Nancy Medford inherit a ranch in New Mexico, they find the majority of their neighbours are hostile to strangers. Befriended by only one rancher, and plagued by rustlers, the thought of returning to England is tempting, but needing to prove himself, Rufus is coached as a fighter by a circus sharp shooter, the mysterious Ghost of the Cimarron. But will this be enough to overcome the frightening odds against him?

GAMBLER'S BULLETS

Robert Lane

The conquering of the American west threw up men with all the virtues and vices. The men of vision, ready to work hard to build a better life, were in the majority. But there were also workshy gamblers, robbers and killers. Amongst these ne'er-do-wells were Melvyn Revett, Trevor Younis and Wilf Murray. But two determined men — Curtis Tyson and Neville Gough — took to the trail, and not until their last bullets were spent would they give up the fight against the lawless trio.

MIDNIGHT LYNCHING

Terry Murphy

When Ruby Malone's husband is lynched by a sheriff's posse, Wells Fargo investigator Asa Harker goes after the beautiful widow expecting her to lead him to the vast sum of money stolen from his company. But Ruby has gone on the outlaw trail with the handsome, young Ben Whitman. Worse still, Harker finds he must deal with a crooked sheriff. Without help, it looks as if he will not only fail to recover the stolen money but also lose his life into the bargain.

BRAZOS STATION

Clayton Nash

Caleb Brett liked his job as deputy sheriff and being betrothed to the sheriff's daughter, Rose. What he didn't like was the thought of the sheriff moving in with them once they were married. But capturing the infamous outlaw Gil Bannerman offered a way out because there was plenty of reward money. Then came Brett's big mistake — he lost Bannerman and was framed. Now everything he treasured was lost. Did he have a chance in hell of fighting his way back?

DEAD IS FOR EVER

Amy Sadler

After rescuing Hope Bennett from the clutches of two trailbums, Sam Carver made a serious mistake. He killed one of the outlaws, and reckoned on collecting the bounty on Lew Daggett. But catching Sam off-guard, Daggett made off with the girl, leaving Sam for dead. However, he was only grazed and once he came to, he set out in search of Hope. When he eventually found her, he was forced into a dramatic showdown with his life on the line.